Eight Days Until Christmas . . .

During math, I wrote Josh this note:

> *My Dad and Miriam are going to New York City on business during Christmas vacation. I'm going too. Want to come?*

Josh looked at the note, looked at me, and wrote back:

> *I'm having Christmas with Jan and George and everyone at the farm. Sorry.*

I couldn't believe it. No one even told me he was having Christmas at our place! I wrote back:

> *We're going the day AFTER Christmas. So do you want to come or not?*

Josh wrote back:

> *Sure. If it's free.*

Was that all the thanks I was getting from Josh Greene for giving him the trip of a lifetime? I must have been crazy to invite him. I wrote back:

> *Don't do me any favors!*

Bantam Skylark Books of related interest
Ask your bookseller for the books you have missed

ANNE OF GREEN GABLES by L.M. Montgomery
THE CHRISTMAS REVOLUTION by Barbara Cohen
DAPHNE'S BOOK by Mary Downing Hahn
THE GHOST IN THE THIRD ROW by Bruce Coville
I WAS A 98-POUND DUCKLING by Jean Van Leeuwen
MISS KNOW IT ALL by Carol Beach York
NOELLE OF THE NUTCRACKER by Pamela Jane
THE PICOLINIS by Anne Graham Estern
YOUR FORMER FRIEND, MATTHEW by LouAnn Gaeddert

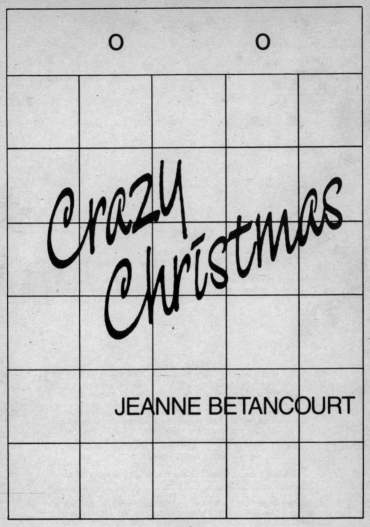

Crazy Christmas

JEANNE BETANCOURT

A BANTAM SKYLARK BOOK®
TORONTO • NEW YORK • LONDON • SYDNEY • AUCKLAND

RL 5, 009–012

CRAZY CHRISTMAS
A Bantam Skylark Book / December 1988

ISBN 0-553-15643-8

Published simultaneously in the United States and Canada

*Bantam Books are published by Bantam Books, a division of
Bantam Doubleday Dell Publishing Group, Inc. Its trademark,
consisting of the words "Bantam Books" and the portrayal of a
rooster, is Registered in U.S. Patent and Trademark Office and
in other countries. Marca Registrada. Bantam Books, 666 Fifth
Avenue, New York, New York 10103.*

PRINTED IN THE UNITED STATES OF AMERICA

CW   0 9 8 7 6 5 4 3 2 1

For my dear aunts—"the Mario Girls"

Catherine Mario Hayden
Marian Mario Parenti
Letitia Mario Bard

ACKNOWLEDGMENTS

Thanks to Paula Flory Bass and her reading classes at Colchester Junior High School for their editorial assistance.

Thanks also to Judy Gitenstein for being almost as interested in Aviva and Josh as I am.

And above all, love and gratitude to Nicole—the original Rainbow Kid—who makes every Crazy Christmas wonderful.

ONE

24 Days Until Christmas

I rolled over on my stomach and looked at the clock. One A.M.—Ugh! I'd been trying to fall asleep for two and a half hours.

Why do we have to move? I asked myself. I love this house so much.

I leaned over the edge of the bed and rubbed my puppy's soft blond fur and woke him up. "Willie," I said, "I've moved about ten thousand times since Mom and Dad split up. That's all I do. Move." He licked my fingers in appreciation of my misery and turned over on his back so I'd rub his belly. I did, and he fell back to sleep. But I was as wide awake as ever.

I lay back on my pillow and got the idea to count the exact number of moves I'd made since my parents got divorced. Maybe *that* would put me to sleep—like counting sheep.

For the past two years I've been a joint-custody kid, so I've lived half the time with my mother in this house and half the time with my father in an apartment. This means that every Monday I move from my mother's house to my father's apartment or from my father's apartment to my mother's house. That's fifty-two moves from the beginning of sixth grade to the beginning of seventh grade. Then fifty-two more moves from the beginning of seventh to the beginning of eighth, which equals 104 moves.

But, I thought, what about sleepaway camp? Then I stayed in one place for eight whole weeks, which comes to only two moves—to and from camp—instead of eight. I was losing track of the numbers so I got up to figure things out on paper.

When I put on the light and looked around, I got more depressed than ever. There were boxes all over my room and smudge marks on the wall where my rainbow poster had hung for so many years. I opened the box marked "Desk Stuff," took out a pad and pencil, and went to work. I finally came up with ninety-four moves, not ten thousand. Even so, it was a lot of times, especially because some moves counted more than others. For instance, just two months ago my dad and I moved out of our own apartment into his girlfriend Miriam's apartment. That was a *big* move.

But the move I was making this morning bothered me the most. Because in a few hours—just twenty-four days before Christmas—my mother Jan, her new husband George, their new baby

Jelo, my dog Willie, my turtle Myrtle, and me—Aviva—were leaving the house I'd lived in practically my whole natural life. We were moving to a run-down place nine miles away on a deserted road outside of town. George and my mom said we needed more room with a baby and everything. I said we should just add another room to the house we already have. Nobody listened to me.

I looked around my own about-to-be-lost-forever room, turned out the light, went back to bed, and counted sheep instead of moves. The last number I remember I don't remember because I was asleep.

"Aviva, wake up. We've got to get this day into high gear." I felt a sticky little hand on my face. I opened my eyes. Mom was holding baby Jelo over me.

"Honey, please watch the baby," she said as she plopped Jelo on my stomach. "The moving van will be here any minute. I have to empty the frig. Or maybe you want to do that and I'll watch the baby?"

I lifted Jelo off my stomach, sat up, put him on my lap, and looked at my mother. "I'm tired, Mom. Please let me sleep. Why can't George empty the refrigerator?" By the time the words were out of my mouth my mother was halfway out of my room. She didn't even turn around when she said, "He's had his applesauce. His bottle's on the bed next to you."

My baby half brother gurgled a smile at me. "Jelo," I said, "why do you have to like me so much?" "Jelo" isn't his real name. It's my nickname for him, because his initials are J.E.L.O. (John Edward Linton O'Connell).

Ten minutes later Jelo was finished with his bottle. I still wasn't dressed, but Willie was hungry and so was I. I figured we'd better eat before Mom finished packing the frig and cabinets. I picked up Jelo, said "Let's go" to Willie, and headed for the kitchen. The first person I saw was Josh Greene stuffing a donut into his mouth. I'd forgotten that he was helping us move.

"You just got up?" he asked. "George and I've been packing the garage since seven o'clock."

I handed him Jelo, grabbed a donut off the kitchen table, and ran out of the room.

"What's wrong with *her*?" I heard Josh ask my mom at the refrigerator.

"Hey, Aviva," George's grown-up daughter Cynthia yelled out to me as I passed her in the living room where she was packing books, "don't say good morning."

"Morning," I called back at her as I went into the bathroom and banged the door shut. George was standing at the sink.

"Oops, sorry," I said as I turned to leave.

"I'm finished," he said. He went past me and out the door. "It's all yours." He was grinning from ear to ear, which looked especially silly because there was still shaving cream around his left ear. "Great day, Aviva. Great day," he said.

Maybe for you, I thought, as I closed the door behind him. You haven't lived in this house practically your whole life.

I looked in the mirror and moaned. Josh saw me looking like *this*! My hair was all over the place—sticking out like I had seen a ghost or was a punk rocker. There were dark circles under my eyes from not getting enough sleep. And I had on this stupid nightgown covered with yellow smile faces whose black outlines had run in the wash. Smiling faces crying black tears.

It isn't that I'm interested in Josh as a boyfriend or anything. We've known each other since first grade. And because we're both the tallest kids in the class, we always end up sitting near each other in the back of the room.

Josh is sort of an orphan. The "sort of" part is that he lives in an orphanage even though his father is alive. George and my mom really like Josh, so our family's always helping him out. Like last year when Josh's father showed up out of nowhere after twelve years, and we had him and Josh come to dinner. Josh's father's a bum, though. A real *bum* bum. A derelict. It's hard to feel sorry for him because he's mean to Josh. Like he's never shown any love for him, his own kid, and he just disappeared when Josh was a year old without any explanation. George says he's probably mentally ill. Anyway, because of all this, George watches out for Josh.

And since Josh sits next to me in school and used to walk my dog Mop, and then gave me Willie after Mop died, you *could* say Josh Greene and I are friends—even though one of us is a girl and the other's a boy. But I hate looking like a mess in front of any of my friends. Which is why when everyone was packing and rushing around, I stayed in the bathroom to take a shower and blow-dry my hair. Then I put my nightgown back on and ran to my room so no one would see me. As I closed the door behind me, I nearly screamed. Two huge men were in my room—piling boxes on a hand truck!

"Sorry, miss," the bigger one said. "Didn't mean to scare you." Before I even started to breathe again, he was giving me orders. "Better clean out that closet, miss. Also there are things under the bed. Put it all in this carton. And what about this?" He pointed to Myrtle's house.

"Leave the turtle there," I said. "I'll be right back and take care of her myself. *Don't* pack her." I grabbed my jeans and sweatshirt from the day before and ran back to the bathroom to get dressed.

First the moving van left. Then George and Josh drove off in George's car with the last of the odds and ends. Then the rest of us left in Mom's car. Willie, Myrtle, and I were in the backseat of the car with Mom's houseplants. Mom and Jelo were up front with Cynthia, who was driving. I turned around to say good-bye to my old wonderful brick house. It looked sad without curtains and plants in the windows. I faced forward and swallowed some hot tears. Mom turned around. There were tears coming down her face. "Good-bye, house," she whispered. I was glad my mother was sad too. I didn't feel so lonely.

Half an hour later we drove up the dirt road to

our new run-down wood-frame farmhouse. Brick houses are a lot stronger. This looked like the kind of house the three little pigs might live in and that a wolf could huff and puff and blow down. I thought, This place will never feel like my home.

By seven o'clock that night, the empty moving van pulled away from Rural Post Office Box 23 and we sat around the dining room table in the big kitchen staring at one another.

Everyone was exhausted, hungry, and crabby. Everyone, that is, except Josh, who'd just come in from a tour of the land and barn and was just plain hungry. "This place is great," he kept repeating. "This place is gr-reat! You've got so much land. This used to be a working farm. Did you see that barn? I mean they used to raise cows and chickens and horses. Picture it. And this house. It's huge!"

"Huge," my mom said, "and drafty." She put Jelo's hat back on even though we were indoors.

George said, "I think we should eat something before we put the beds together."

"Let's order in pizza," I suggested. "Or Chinese food."

"They don't deliver out here," George said.

"What?" I shouted. "We've left civilization. No pizza, no Chinese food? It's like being on a deserted island here."

"I'll make some chili," Cynthia said. She started rummaging through the boxes marked "Food." "There's ground beef from the freezer, it should be thawed out by now."

She plopped a box of crackers on the table and a container of juice. "Have these for a snack, and by the time you put the beds together, dinner will be ready."

My mom smiled up at her. "I'm so glad you're moving in with us," she said. "You're a treasure."

This is the deal with Cynthia. She's in graduate school at the University of Vermont studying nutrition, which is probably why she likes to cook. In order for us to afford the farm, she's living with us instead of having to pay rent in town. Which means George saves money because he'd have to pay rent for her, since she's his daughter and still a student. Otherwise, George said, we couldn't have afforded to buy the house until after she graduated. And by then this house would be sold. I remember thinking, So what? Maybe we could have just passed up this house. But I didn't say that to George.

By the time we'd put the beds together and had dinner, I was ready to collapse. But Josh was still there, sort of hanging around. You could tell he didn't want to go back to St. Joseph's Home. Every time George would say they'd better get going, Josh would find something else to do. Finally, while we were all sort of just sitting around the dinner table, too tired to even get up, George said, "You know, Josh, I don't think I can face that drive back to town tonight. Would you mind too much sleeping over? Maybe help me out tomorrow too." George looked around at the boxes and general

8

disorder. "You'd be kind of roughing it tonight, though."

Josh looked up from playing with Willie. They were the only two who had any energy left. "I don't mind, if Father Tierney says it's okay," Josh said in this very grown-up way when I knew he really wanted to jump up and down and shout, "Whoopee. I'd love to sleep over. That's what I wanted to do all along. I love it here."

That's when I went up the rickety stairs to bed.

This is what my so-called new bedroom was like: awful. It had old water-stained, pink-and-yellow-flowered wallpaper; it had plaster falling off the ceiling; it had faded black and green linoleum that had sticky black streaks where it was worn through. And the windows rattled even when there was barely any wind, like there was a ghost or something trying to get in.

George and my mother said we had to renovate the whole house. Since the rest of the place was as bad as my room, I figured I'd be ready for college by the time they got to me. I unrolled my sleeping bag from camp and put it on my mattress.

As I was dropping off to sleep I thought I heard George and Josh whistling "Old MacDonald Had a Farm." It made sense that Josh would love all this farm business because he wants to be a veterinarian when he grows up. In fact, Myrtle is his turtle. I'm just taking care of her until he has a place of his own. Josh says that since turtles can live for hundreds of years, he'll still have plenty of time to spend with Myrtle.

"The first week in a new place is bound to be confusing," my mom said to me a couple of days later when I'd missed the school bus home and she and Jelo had to come all the way into town to pick me up. "When we get back to the farm you're going to have to help with Jelo so I can make dinner."

"It's not my fault I missed the bus," I said. "I was helping Sister Bernard Marie. And when I get home I have to . . ."

Mom went right on talking over what I was saying. "Maybe what you need is one of those watches with a timer that will ring when it's time for the bus. How much do you think they cost?"

Jelo started to fuss. I stuck the yellow pacifier in his mouth. "I dunno," I said. "I guess about thirty, forty dollars."

My mother looked disappointed. "Too much," she said. She glanced at me. "You know, Aviva, with my not going back to work at the phone company and the big mortgage on the farm, things are a little tight now moneywise."

I stared out the window as we drove out of town toward the hills. "I didn't ask for anything, Mom. You had the idea about the watch. And why do you call it 'the farm'? It's not like we're raising animals or crops or anything."

I was missing my old house.

Sunday I didn't finish my homework until after ten-thirty and I had to get up at six-thirty the next morning to be ready for the school bus pickup at seven-thirty.

I went out into the hall to the top of the stairs. I could hear George trying to teach *my* puppy how to fetch. "Go ahead, Willie," he was coaching. "Get the ball."

"Willie," I yelled. "Come here. It's time for bed."

"Go to Aviva, Willie," George ordered.

No Willie.

I went halfway down the stairs and yelled again, "Come on, Willie."

I could hear George laughing. "He did it, Aviva," he yelled to me. "He brought me the ball." Then to Willie he said, "Good pup. Let's do it again."

I turned around without saying anything and headed back up the stairs.

"Good night, Aviva," George called. "Willie will be there in a little while."

"Good night," I called back.

I went to the door of Jelo's room. My mother was standing over his crib. She was singing, "Hush, little baby, don't you cry . . ." in her soft voice, just like she always used to sing it to me. She didn't see me. I said, "Good night, Mom."

She turned toward me in the dim light of Jelo's clown lamp and, without even missing a note, put her finger to her lips to tell me not to make any noise.

I closed the door and headed down the hall. Cynthia's door was partway opened. "Good night, Cynthia," I called through the crack.

"Just a second," I heard her say. Then she called back to me, "Good night, Aviva," and went right on talking on the phone.

11

Well, I thought, tomorrow night I'll be sleeping at Dad and Miriam's and it looks like no one on "the farm" will even notice that I'm gone.

I was the first person the school bus picked up in the mornings. Even though the bus driver, Lillian, is old enough to be somebody's grandmother, she has curly dyed blond hair, wears overalls, and always has on bright orangy-red lipstick. "How you doing this morning, girlie?" she asked as I got on board.

"Okay," I said. "I won't be here the rest of this week, though, so you don't have to leave so early." As the bus rattled along through the misty early morning light to the next stop, I told her about my joint custody, how I lived one week with my mother, then one week with my father. Back and forth, back and forth.

"Sounds pretty confusing to me," she said.

"It's all right," I said.

I didn't tell her I was looking forward to being at my dad's so I could stay in bed an hour later every morning. I didn't want her to think I didn't like her bus or something.

"So where's your suitcase?" she asked.

"My mom'll drop off my suitcase and my dog at my dad's place, when she goes to Burlington to go food shopping this afternoon."

Most of the kids on the bus went to public school. There were only about five of us from St. Agnes and only one of them was in my class. That was Rita. But she was the last one to get on the bus, so it didn't help much.

The way I figured it, Rita could get up when I got on the bus and still have time to take a shower, get dressed, have breakfast, and even do a little homework before she got picked up.

No way was I ever going to like living so far away from town.

TWO

15 Days Until Christmas

I went to my dad and Miriam's right after school so I'd be there when Mom came with Willie and my stuff. As I walked down the block I checked one more time to be sure I had my key.

Miriam's condominium is about a mile from my school. Very convenient for me. And since the university where my father teaches is just up the hill from the condominium, it's convenient for him too. All of the apartments are alike, which is okay because they're nice. Everything is clean and new. The bottom floors—like Miriam's—have little fenced-in backyards and the second floors have decks. It's the kind of place where if the climate were warmer, they'd have a swimming pool.

I unlocked the door, went in, turned on the lights, and took a deep breath. Miriam's place has this special smell. It's the same smell that she uses in her store—like a bouquet of spring flowers. She puts drops of flower oil on her light bulbs and when you turn on the lights, the air fills with the smell of flowers.

I put down my bookbag and walked around. It was so peaceful and organized at Miriam's. I flipped on the stereo, changed the station from classical music to rock and roll, and went into my room. It's about a third of the size of my room at the farm. I don't mind because it's new and fresh-looking. Miriam put up lace curtains and got me sheets and a quilt in a tiny pink flower design. Since Dad and I moved in with Miriam in September, each time I come back from a MOM week there's something new in my room. Sometimes it's something to wear from Miriam's store, like the pink flannel nightgown. Or something new for my room, like the yellow rug and the blue towels. Other weeks it's a little thing, like a pen or a pack of stickers. But last time it was the biggest yet—my own extension phone, shaped like a banana. I love it.

My present for this week was a bouquet of daisies in a vase on my desk. A small envelope was propped against the vase. I wondered who had the idea to give me flowers—Miriam or my dad. I opened the envelope. The note was in my dad's handwriting!

> *Welcome home,*
> *Aviva.*
>
> *Love,*
>
> *Dad and Miriam*

I let out a deep breath and smiled. It was good to be back.

The doorbell rang. Mom. I ran to the door and opened it. She stood there holding my suitcase, Willie on a leash, and a crying Jelo. "Help!" she said.

She let go of the leash, and Willie started jumping all over me. I picked him up. "What's wrong with Jelo?" I asked.

"Dirty diaper. Hungry. The whole works." She looked frazzled.

"Do you want to come in?" I asked.

This is where being a divorced kid can get complicated. My mom and dad don't fight anymore, but they hardly ever see each other or go in each other's houses. The only time they talk is when it's about me—and that's usually done on the phone. I knew for a fact that Mom had never been inside Miriam's apartment.

Jelo's crying got louder.

"Maybe I'd better come in," she said. "Just for a minute."

She followed me into the living room. "It smells nice in here, like flowers."

"But Jelo stinks," I said, as she laid him out on the couch to change his diaper.

While she changed him I put my suitcase in my room and gave Willie some water.

"You want some tea or something?" I yelled from the kitchen.

"What time do they get home?" she asked.

"Sometimes Dad comes right from the university and sometimes he helps Miriam at the store until she closes."

"Do you have juice or something that won't take time?" she asked.

"Tea doesn't take time," I explained. "With the microwave."

"Of course," she said. "The microwave." She looked around. "Aviva, this place is right out of *House Beautiful* magazine or something. It's so new and *neat*. Nothing is out of place. It's hard to believe your father lives here."

"Dad's changed," I said.

"I can see." She sighed. "You must love it after our place."

"I liked our house," I told her. "I mean our old house."

We sat on the couch while she nursed Jelo and drank her tea. I prayed she'd be gone before Miriam and Dad got home. And she was.

After Mom and Jelo left I unpacked my suitcase, called my best friend Sue on my banana phone, fed Willie, and did my homework while I watched a

17

M*A*S*H rerun. Dad and Miriam got home about seven, just as I was choosing between starving to death or ruining my appetite for dinner with a fluffer-nutter sandwich.

"Hey, hey," Dad said when I met him at the door. We gave each other a big hug.

"Hi, Aviva. Hungry?" Miriam held out a brown shopping bag. "How does Chinese sound? Got your favorite."

"Sesame noodles," I squealed. "Oh, yeah, and thanks for the flowers. They're great."

"Not as great as you are," Dad said.

"What smells?" Miriam asked as she sniffed the air in all directions.

I was about to tell her about Jelo's dirty diaper when I saw, out of the corner of my eye, a Willie plop in the middle of the kitchen floor. So did Miriam.

"Sorry," I said. As I went for the paper towels I saw Miriam glare at my dad.

"He's just a puppy," my dad explained. "He's had a lot of changes in the last few days. He'll straighten out in no time."

"He'd better," Miriam whispered to my dad. She didn't think I heard her, but I did.

In another few minutes everything was back to peaceful at Miriam's and we were sitting around the table eating sesame noodles and chicken with snow peas.

"Well, Aviva," Dad said as he gave Miriam a mischievous look. "We have two surprises. One is about me and one is"—he pointed a chopstick at me—"about you. Start guessing."

"About me or about you?" I asked.

"Let's start with me," he said. "I'll give you a hint." He started chanting in a sing-song voice, "No more pencils. No more books. No more teacher's dirty looks."

"I don't get it," I said.

He continued the chant with his own words, "No more piles of papers to correct, no more faculty meetings."

"You're quitting teaching?" I asked.

He grinned and nodded yes as Miriam leaned over and gave him a big kiss on the cheek. "Isn't he wonderful?" she said.

"Why?" I asked. "I thought you liked being a professor and having the summers off and everything."

"It's time for a change." He smiled at Miriam. "And my half of the money from the sale of the house is giving me the chance."

"What are you going to do?" I asked. I'd forgotten all about my sesame noodles.

"Open a men's boutique in the shopping mall. Right next to Miriam's Magic. I signed the lease today. And do you know what it's going to be called?" he asked. "Granger's Town and Country."

"That's great, Dad," I said, even though I wasn't sure that it was.

"And what about Aviva's surprise?" Miriam asked.

I was so surprised about Dad's surprise that I'd forgotten that I had a surprise too. I was sure it wasn't that I could quit school.

"Okay," Dad said, "here's your hint." He held the chopsticks up to his mouth like a microphone and sang the opening bars of a song.

"New York, New York," I said in a hushed voice. "Am I going to visit New York City?"

"Yes!" he boomed. "New York, New York. Between Christmas and the New Year. I'll be finished with teaching—for good—so Miriam and I are going on a buying trip for both stores."

"Tell her the rest," Miriam said.

"You can bring a friend," Dad said. "So you'll have someone to go around with in the city while we're working. We'll plan tours and things for you to do and she'll share your room and be our guest."

"Wow," I said. "I can't believe it. New York City. I always wanted to go to New York. I mean, I'll finally see everything." I looked down at my plate of noodles, "Like Chinatown and . . . and . . . the Statue of Liberty and the Empire State Building and . . ." I looked at my puppy sleeping in the kitchen, "the Bronx Zoo and . . ."

My dad continued, "The Christmas tree at Rockefeller Center and . . ."

Miriam picked it up. "And the Rockettes at Radio City Music Hall . . . and Central Park."

I jumped up and gave them both kisses. "It's the best present," I said. "Thank you."

"So who are you going to bring?" Dad asked.

"That's easy," Miriam said. "Sue, of course. She's her best friend."

"Yeah," I said. "Of course."

After helping with the dishes and walking Willie I sat on the edge of my bed and picked up my banana to call Sue and invite her to come to New York City with me. But when she picked up at the other end, I decided there was no rush in telling her about the trip, so I asked her a question about the history homework instead. The truth was I wasn't sure she was the very best person to take. Sue is shy and gets scared easily. Being on our own in New York would be an adventure and I wanted to be with someone who was adventurous.

Maybe, I thought, after I hung up, I should invite Louise. She acts and looks the oldest of all my girlfriends. She even dates a high school boy. Or Rita. She went to New York City to visit her uncle last year. That'd be neat, to go with someone who'd been there before. Sue, Louise, or Rita? I couldn't decide who to invite. Well, I thought, the important thing is that I am going to New York—and will be flying on a plane for the first time in my life. What a Christmas present!

Christmas presents. I went to my desk and wrote down the names of all the people I had to buy Christmas presents for. Christmas was a little over two weeks away. I'd been so busy with moving that I hadn't started my Christmas shopping. I'd have to get something extra special for Miriam and Dad.

This is how the rest of the school week went:

Tuesday Willie went on the kitchen floor again, but I got it cleaned up before Miriam got home.

Wednesday Willie turned over the wastebasket and there was garbage and chewed-up newspapers all over the living room.

Thursday I closed Willie in the bathroom while I was at school. When I got home I found he'd been in the bathtub all day. He'd climbed on the edge of the tub, fallen in, and then couldn't get out. "I'm sorry," I said, picking him up. "You must be so bored and lonely here all day."

I let him sit on the couch with me while I watched TV, even though it was against Miriam's rules. Then I took him for the longest walk ever, even though it was raining.

The first thing Miriam said when she got home was, "What smells?"

"I don't smell anything," I answered.

She sniffed some more. "Phew," she said as she pointed an accusing finger at my wet puppy. She glared at my dad. "It's his fur. It smells awful. Don't you ever bathe him? That's a very annoying odor."

I was pretty annoyed with Miriam. Some people are too fussy.

The next day in homeroom I passed Josh this note:

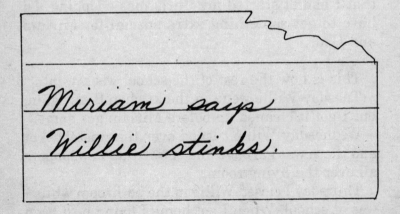

Miriam says
Willie stinks.

In a few minutes Josh handed this back.

ROSES R RED

VIOLETS R BLUE.

DOGS HAVE A SMELL

PEOPLE DO 2.

P.S. How does Miriam's
breath smell when she
wakes up in the morning?

I couldn't help it. I giggled. Mrs. Petronella Peterson tried to stop me with a stern, "Miss Granger." But I couldn't stop.

I was still laughing when I said, "I'm sorry, Mrs. Peterson. I can't help it."

She glowered at me. "I see. Well, you can help me after school with cleaning the blackboards and waxing the desks."

Mrs. P. P. is the only teacher I've had who cleans and waxes the top of each and every desk twice a week. Actually *she* doesn't do it—a student does. And Friday that student was me, which meant I didn't get home until four-thirty, hours after Miriam had left for work without closing her bedroom door and I don't know how long after Willie had peed in the middle of her bed.

I called Josh at Angelo's Animal Care where he works after school. "Josh," I shrieked. "Willie peed on Miriam's bed. Through everything. Her feather quilt with the lace edge, the sheets, the mattress. Josh, stop laughing. You've got to help me. You gave me this dumb dog."

"Do you have a washing machine?" he asked.

"Yes. The sheets are in it now. But I can't wash the quilt and what about the mattress?"

"I'll ask Angelo if I can leave early," he said. "We'll figure something out." Before he hung up he asked, "How's Willie?"

"Sleeping," I said. I didn't tell Josh that I'd screamed at my dog and hit him for the first time ever. I felt awful. After all, it wasn't Willie's fault that he was alone all day.

The first thing Josh did when he got to Miriam's was eat a fluffer-nutter sandwich and play with Willie. Then we went into Miriam and my dad's bedroom and faced the stinky mattress and quilt. There was this big brownish yellow stain in the middle of the blue-and-white-flowered quilt and—worst of all—a matching stain soaked into the middle of the mattress.

"Get some water and ammonia," Josh ordered in his all-business veterinarian voice. "And a scrub brush."

"You can't wash it," I said. "You'll get the mattress wet."

"It's wet already," he observed. "Do you have one of those hair dryer blower things?"

As Josh was scrubbing the mattress and as I was blow-drying where he'd cleaned the quilt, I said, "The stain didn't come out of the quilt."

"No problem," Josh said as he finished his work and sat back to watch me do mine. "Just turn it over after you dry it. The same pattern's on both sides."

"She'll see it someday," I said. "And what about the smell?" I took a sniff of the mattress. "It still stinks."

"What about that oil stuff you told me she puts on the light bulbs?" he asked.

Sometimes I think Josh Greene is the smartest kid I know.

Half an hour later we stood at the door of the bedroom and surveyed our work. "Not bad," Josh said.

"It smells pretty," I said. "And it looks normal."

We closed the door. Josh emptied the bucket of water and ammonia and I put the bottle of oil back in the end-table drawer.

"Well, I gotta go," Josh said. "See ya. I'm working on the farm tomorrow."

"How come?"

"George hired me to help him set up his tools and stuff in the barn."

"I'm working at Miriam's store tomorrow," I said. "Wrapping presents for Christmas shoppers.

Besides," I added, "it's still a DAD week until Monday."

"Okay," Josh said as he opened the door to go. "See ya."

"Josh," I asked. "You ever been to New York City?"

"Me?" he said. "Nah. It's supposed to be fun, though. Going to New York City would be an adventure. You know, like exploring a strange place. I mean compared to Burlington, Vermont, New York is like a foreign country. You going there or something?"

"Yeah. Sometime."

"Well, me too. I'm going *sometime*," he said.

"Thanks, again," I said. "For helping. You probably saved my life, or at least Willie's."

"Well, he's safe until she turns the quilt cover over," he said.

After Josh left, I thought it would be a lot more fun to go around New York with him than with Sue or Louise or Rita. It's too bad Josh is a guy.

The first thing Miriam said when she walked into the apartment that night was, "What do I smell?"

I was pretending to do my homework at the dining room table. "I don't smell anything," I said without looking up. "I put some of that oil stuff on the light bulb. Maybe that's it."

She laughed. "You used too much. All it takes is a drop."

"Oh," I said. "I didn't know." I sure didn't. We'd used half a bottle on her mattress.

"I'm exhausted," she said to my dad. "I'm going to put on my robe." I held my breath as she headed toward her room and opened the door.

"What?" she yelled. "What's been going on here?" She came right back and faced me. "Aviva, my bedroom smells like . . . like I don't know what. Ammonia or something, and that flower oil. What happened?"

I swallowed hard and looked imploringly at my dad.

"Aviva," he said. "What did you do?"

"It's not my fault," I said to Miriam. "You left the door to your room open when you went to work this morning."

After I told them about Willie's accident, they went into the bedroom and looked at the other side of the quilt and the mattress. Dad kept making excuses for Willie and me, and Miriam kept biting her lips to keep from losing her temper.

I said, "Willie doesn't get into so much trouble at Mom's."

"That's because someone's there all day and he has plenty of room to run around," my dad explained.

"Well, then," Miriam said sharply, "maybe he'd better just stay there."

I didn't say anything. I picked Willie up and went to my room. I could hear Dad and Miriam arguing in whispers. I wondered if there was a home for girls the way there was a home for boys, and if Willie and I shouldn't just go there to live.

THREE
10 Days Until Christmas

Saturday morning the world, at least the Vermont part of it, was covered with eight inches of snow. It was the first real snowfall of the winter and the best kind for sledding and skiing. By the time I got up and saw this, Miriam and Dad were already dressed and having breakfast.

Miriam acted like she hadn't been furious with Willie and me the night before. She was all excited about how many Christmas shoppers would be going to her store. "You might think," she was telling my dad and me, "that people would stay home or go play in the snow, but what'll happen is the snow will put them in the Christmas spirit, and once they're in the spirit they'll realize how much shopping they have to do and come to my store."

"And," I added, "they'll want their presents wrapped."

"I wanted to talk to you about that," Miriam said as she cast a suspicious eye at Willie sniffing around her feet. "I think we have a problem here. I don't think you should leave Willie alone today."

"Maybe you can work in the store after school on the days when Willie stays at your mom's," Dad said.

"But there aren't as many people shopping during the week and I have to take the school bus right after school. Besides, I need to make money to buy *my* Christmas presents." And, I thought, my friends are coming by the store to see me and I won't be there.

Half an hour later they were off to open the store and I was left behind with Willie. It was his first big snow, which was great fun for him. But by eleven o'clock we were back indoors and I was pretty bored. I was about to call Sue when the phone rang.

"Hi, honey." It was Mom. "Listen, I'm at the supermarket in town. You want to come out to the farm for the afternoon? It's so beautiful out there with the snow and everything. A gorgeous day. And Willie could probably use the exercise."

When she said that, I knew my dad must have called and told her about Willie wetting the bed.

"Sure," I said, thinking anything would be better than being cooped up in this apartment and having to be so careful not to mess it up. "But we have to be home for supper," I told her. "It's still a DAD week."

"Fine," she said. "I'll pick you up in five minutes. Listen for the horn."

I hung up the phone and picked it up again to call my dad and tell him.

He was all excited about the Christmas shoppers. "Boy, Aviva, it's popping here. Customers all over the place. And we're telling them all about Granger's Town and Country. Everyone thinks it's a great idea. What's up with you?"

That's when I got this idea. "Mom invited me out to her place to see it in the snow and everything, but maybe she could take Willie and I could come to the store and work. What do you think?"

He thought that was a terrific plan and added an idea of his own. "Why doesn't Willie stay at your mother's until you go back on Monday. That way you can work at the store tomorrow, too."

I didn't like the idea of being separated from my puppy for so long, but it did make sense. "Just this once," I said. "Remember, you and Miriam both said I could have a dog at your place. He'll behave better when he gets older. You said so yourself."

"I know," Dad said. "It's just crazy now with the holidays. It's up to you. Do you want to work or not?"

"I'm just saying . . ."

"I know what you're saying, Aviva. Now I have to get back to work. Hurry. We need you."

I changed into a skirt and sweater that I thought made me look older and put on some of Miriam's makeup. I was snapping on Willie's leash when I heard the horn honk.

"My, aren't we all dressed up," my mom said when I got into the car.

"I have a favor to ask," I said as I banged the

door shut. "Could you dog-sit for Willie and drop me off at the mall? Dad and Miriam need me to wrap presents for customers at the store. You know, because of all the Christmas shoppers. You might think they wouldn't be out because of the snow, but they're out more than ever. You see the snow puts people in the Christmas spirit, which reminds them that they have a lot of shopping left. And they all want their presents wrapped. Which is what I do. And I need to do it because—"

My mom put her hand on my arm. "Hey, slow down. I'll take care of Willie. I'd rather go sledding with you, but I understand."

"Besides," I said. "It's a DAD week anyway."

As we pulled away from the curb and headed through the snowy streets to downtown and the mall, I looked around the car. "Where's Jelo?"

"Josh's watching him."

"Oh," I said. "Well, tell him I said hi."

"Okay," she said. "It's nice to see you two getting along so well."

"Jelo," I corrected her. "Tell Jelo hi, not Josh."

She smiled at me. "Sure."

Then I remembered. "I can't believe I forgot to tell you, Mom. Guess what Dad and Miriam are giving me for Christmas?"

"A puppy."

"Very funny."

"Two puppies."

"No. Listen, Mom." And I tried to sing her "New York, New York," the way Dad did. When I ran out of lyrics, I said, "Guess."

"Your father already told me," she admitted. "I

think it's a great present. I'm just not sure I like the idea of two girls being on their own all day in New York. It's a lot more complicated than finding your way around Burlington. I don't know."

"Oh, Mom, it'll be fine. Dad'll give us directions and we won't go far. He said we can take cabs every place and that he'll pay for it."

"What does Sue's mother say about all this? Has Roy talked to her?"

She braked the car in front of the mall and we faced each other. "I didn't ask Sue yet. I mean I don't know if I want to."

"If you don't invite Sue, who would you invite? She's your best friend."

After a moment of silence we said in unison, "Josh."

"Josh would be loads of fun on a trip like that," Mom said. Then she started to laugh. She almost couldn't stop.

"What's so funny?" I asked. Sometimes she's so weird.

"Well," she said through giggles, "what will you do about sleeping arrangements at the hotel?"

My heart sank. I couldn't share a hotel room with Josh. "I guess it's not such a good idea after all."

"Oh, it's not impossible," Mom said. "It just means you'd share a room with Miriam, and Roy would share a room with Josh." And she started up laughing again. "Not too romantic for the love-birds."

That's when I decided for sure I'd invite Josh

Greene to come to New York City with me.

I leaned over and kissed my mother good-bye. "Thanks for taking care of Willie." I opened the car door and got out. "See you Monday."

"Don't miss the school bus home," she said as she turned on the motor and I waved good-bye to my puppy, who I wouldn't see for two whole days.

The instant I stepped on the escalator to go from the street into the underground mall, I knew that Miriam was right about the shoppers getting into the Christmas spirit. I'd never seen the mall so crowded. They were playing "White Christmas" over the P.A. system, and every store window was decorated for the season. By the time I got to the front of Miriam's Magic, I was filled with the spirit myself.

Miriam's window display was the prettiest of all. It had a real Christmas tree decorated in only gold ornaments. Even the tiny lights were gold-colored. Under the tree were piles of opened presents, with pretty wrappings around them. All gifts from Miriam's Magic. Standing next to the tree were a woman mannequin in a pink silk robe and a man mannequin in a navy blue wool robe. The man was handing a beautifully wrapped box to the woman, who was hiding a box for him behind her back. The whole display was called "The Magic of Christmas."

Through the window I could see a bunch of people shopping in the store, with only Miriam and my dad to help them. I went in.

Dad was at the cash register putting a lady's package in a Miriam's Magic bag. When our eyes met, he said to his customer, "Ma'am, how would you like your purchase gift-wrapped, compliments of the store?" He motioned with his head toward me. "Our wrapper has just arrived."

"Why my, yes," the customer said. "That would be lovely."

Dad had set up a card table for me in the back of the store. There were scissors and tape and ribbons neatly laid out along one side, and on the floor next to the table there was a big box with dozens of rolls of gorgeous paper. The kind of paper I always wanted to buy, but never could because it's so expensive. Shiny, thick papers with holiday designs. All very sophisticated. All very Miriam.

I would rather have been in the front of the store so I could see the action in the main part of the mall, but Miriam said that the back was better because to get something wrapped, a customer would have to walk through the whole store two more times—once from the cash register to the wrapping table and once to get to the exit. She said they might decide to buy something else during these trips.

I'm a really good wrapper, but I've never done it with people watching or saying, "On second thought maybe a red bow would be better than a green one. Would you mind terribly changing it?" Or, "How long will I have to wait?" I also wasn't used to wrapping with two people waiting their turn while the person I'm helping can't decide which paper he wants.

This is what I didn't have my first day of being a Christmas-present wrapper: patience or lunch.

I was in the middle of the last knot of a red *and* green ribbon on gold shooting-star paper when I heard, "Hey, there she is." I looked up. It was Rita and Louise. They came up on either side of me and watched with my customer as I gave the knot a last tug.

I handed it to the customer, who said, "Do you really think the red and green look good together? Maybe it should be red and gold."

"I think it looks fabulous," I said.

The two people waiting mumbled in agreement, but Louise said, "Maybe red and gold would be prettier. You know, with the gold paper." I moved my foot around and kicked Louise's leg.

"Do you really?" the customer asked.

"I . . . I was just kidding," Louise said. "I think it looks great."

"Besides," I said. "There are people waiting."

I flexed my fingers and shifted in the chair. I was stiff from sitting so long and had about four thousand paper cuts on my hands. I looked up at my friends before I began the next gift. "Hi, guys," I said.

"This is so neat," Louise said.

"You're so lucky," Rita said.

"Aviva," Miriam called. "Could you come here a minute." She was near the dressing room waiting for the customer inside.

I pushed my chair back and got up. "I'll be right back," I said to my three customers and two friends. I pointed to the box of wrapping paper. "Why don't you pick out your paper?"

When I reached Miriam, her pleasant-salesperson smile turned into a scowl. "Two things," she whispered. "I saw the last package go out. No double ribbons. If you do it for one, you'll have to do it for all. That stuff's costing me. And *no* socializing. Tell your friends they can see you during your break."

"When will that be?" I asked. My stomach was reminding me that it'd been ages since I'd eaten anything.

"Let's see." She looked at her watch. "We close at nine. It's four now. I'd say around five. Just put up a sign on your desk, 'Back at five-thirty.'"

The customer she was waiting for came out of the dressing room in a red blouse and black satin pants. In an instant Miriam turned her big scowl for me into a big smile for the customer. "My," Miriam gushed, "that is smashing on you. I've been waiting for someone to try that combination. Well, it's just as I thought—perfect. I hope it's not a gift, because it looks wonderful on you." Miriam grabbed my arm as I was turning to leave. "Isn't it just perfect, Aviva?"

I managed a smile. "It's beautiful," I said. And I went back toward my wrapping desk, where Louise and Rita were helping my customers decide which combination of ribbons to use. Rita was saying, "Maybe three together. Like this gold ribbon with the red and green ribbons."

I took a deep breath and thought of Willie and Josh and Cynthia playing in the snow. That's when I remembered Jelo. It was his first winter and his first big snow and I wasn't even there to see if he liked it or not.

This is how many presents I wrapped from noon on Saturday until eight P.M. on Sunday: 103. This is how much money I made: $80.50.

FOUR

8 Days Until Christmas

When the alarm went off Monday morning I rolled over and moaned, "Oh no, Willie. I can't get up. Never, ever. Just five more minutes." I hung over the side of the bed and waited for his wet kisses. When I opened my eyes I realized that Willie was at my mom's and that since I was going there myself after school, I'd better get up and pack my stuff.

Josh was already in his seat when I rushed to my place about one second before the late bell rang. "You do the history homework?" he asked the instant I sat down.

"No," I said. "Didn't you?"

"You always do it." He looked at me like I'd committed a crime. "I was depending on you."

He opened his history book. "I don't even know what it was about."

"Immigration," I said. "You know, all kinds of people moving to America."

During the day's announcements over the loudspeaker, and then while Mrs. P. P. wrote some notes on the board, I did the first three homework questions and Josh did the last three. And Mrs. P. P. didn't call on either of us or collect the homework. But she did mention New York City about ten thousand times during her lesson on immigration to America—all the oppressed people of the world who found a haven in America, starting out in New York. And I was going to see the Statue of Liberty that they saw as they approached America's shores and freedom. And this very day I was going to give the gift of New York to the poor soul who sat next to me in school—Josh Greene, who was practically an orphan. I felt like a saint, about to grant a great gift. It was so satisfying to do good works. During math, I wrote Josh this note:

My dad and Miriam are going to New York City on business during Christmas vacation. I'm going too. Want to come?

Josh looked at the note, looked at me, and wrote
back:

I'm having Christmas with
Jan and George and
everyone at the farm.
Sorry.

I couldn't believe it. No one even told me he was
having Christmas at our place! I wrote back:

We're going the day
AFTER Christmas. So
do you want to
come or not?

Josh wrote back:

SURE.

IF IT'S FREE.

Was that all the thanks I was getting from Josh Greene for giving him the trip of a lifetime? I must have been crazy to invite him. I wrote back:

Don't do me any favors!

He read that note and gave me a blank look. I ignored Josh for the rest of the morning. I was thinking I should have invited Sue after all. She'd appreciate a trip to New York City and get all excited. It would be more fun to plan the trip with Sue. We could talk about what clothes to bring and stuff like that. The only thing Josh Greene ever wore was dungarees and T-shirts.

When the bell rang for lunch I started up the aisle and yelled out to Sue to wait up.

"Hey, Aviva," Josh said to my back. "Don't tell anybody."

I turned to him and whispered, "Of course not. What do you think I am, crazy? Don't you, either."

Then he whispered back, "How are we getting there?"

"On a plane, of course."

His eyes lit up and he grinned so big I thought he'd split his face. "We're flying?" he asked in a husky whisper.

"Yeah."

"All right!" he shouted. "All right!" Then he took three big strides down the aisle to catch up with Ron Cioffi.

"What was that all about?" Sue asked as we left the room for the cafeteria.

"Nothing," I said. "Josh probably passed a math test or something."

After lunch we had Sister Bernard Marie's class. She's my favorite teacher of all time and our eighth-grade English teacher. This is what I like about Sister Bernard Marie: She makes everyone feel like they're special—even Ronnie Cioffi, who's the only kid in our class who still hasn't outgrown being a troublemaker. I also like her nun's habit. It's the old-fashioned kind with a black skirt that brushes the floor and a black veil and a white thing like a bib and giant rosary beads that hang from her belt. She's neat.

She had a big smile, as usual. "Class," she said, "now that we've read *West Side Story,* it's time to read the play that *West Side Story* was based on, Shakespeare's *Romeo and Juliet*."

The whole class moaned because we'd heard that Shakespeare was hard.

"No need for that," she said, still smiling. "It's the most famous love story of all time." Now the whole class giggled. "I'm sure you'll all do just fine and we'll have a wonderful time with my friend, Will Shakespeare. Now, Aviva and Josh, would you please go to my room? I've left the books on the desk. Mr. Jackson is teaching in there, but he's expecting you."

"Yes, Sister," I said as I pushed my chair back and got up.

"Sure," Josh said.

As we were leaving the room I heard Sister announce, "Now the rest of us will get back our final essays on *West Side Story*."

More moans.

As soon as we were in the hall I told Josh, "I'm going to tell my friends I'm going to New York City, but I'm not telling them anyone's coming with me."

"I'm going to say I'm working on the farm with George during vacation," Josh said.

"Oh," I said.

"You should have seen Willie in the snow yesterday," Josh said. "He kept sinking in and jumping out. He was like an acrobat. And he'd rub his nose, his whole face in it and roll over. He just loved it."

"I know," I said. "I took him for a walk Saturday morning."

43

"Jan told me Willie's staying there, even when you're at your dad's. That's probably a good idea because there's so much room for him to run around."

"That's not a permanent arrangement," I said. "It's just for the holidays, while I'm working."

We'd reached Mr. Jackson's room. Everyone was at strict attention copying math problems off the board. Josh opened the door and walked right up to the desk.

"Sister Bernard Marie told us to pick up the books," he said.

Mr. Jackson doesn't believe in smiling during school hours, so he nodded at us instead. I said "Thank you" and we both took an armful of books and went back to the hall. Josh and I never pass notes during our science class with Mr. Jackson.

"How did Jelo like the snow?" I asked.

"He loved it," Josh said. "Jan has this old sled with sides on it." *My sled,* I thought, from when I was a baby. But I didn't tell Josh. He was going on and on about Jelo and the snow. "We bundled him up in a big blanket and I pulled him. He laughed and laughed."

I thought about how cute Jelo was getting. When he was first born he looked like a Cabbage Patch Kid, but now he looked like the pictures of me when I was a baby. I could imagine him in the snow—his little puffy cheeks all red in the cold. And he'd make that deep gurgly sound, like he was about to blow bubbles. I wondered if I'd be the one to teach Jelo how to blow spit bubbles or

44

whether Josh would do that too. "Wasn't it too cold?" I asked.

"Nah. But here's the best part. I told you how Willie was jumping and everything. Well, he'd never jump near Jelo like you'd expect with a puppy. You know, you'd think he'd run right next to the sled and get snow all over Jelo, or even jump on the sled. He did when I was pulling the sled empty. But the incredible thing is he didn't when Jelo was in it. It was like he was protecting the baby. Willie's a very smart dog and you can tell he loves Jelo."

"He doesn't seem very smart about mattresses," I said. Then I said, "I thought you went there to work with George."

"I did," he said, "in the mornings."

"You stayed over?"

"'Course. I mean because I was working two days." This was ridiculous. Josh Greene was spending more time with my mother than I was.

"Don't you work at Angelo's veterinarian place anymore?"

"That's just during the week now," Josh said. "Angelo said I should help George for as long as he needs it."

"I see," I said. But I didn't. I didn't see why Josh, who was my friend first, was spending all this time with *my* mother, *my* half brother, *my* dog, in *my* house—when I wasn't even there.

As Lillian's school bus rumbled to the stop at the foot of our road, I thought: The first thing I'm going to do at Mom's is take a nap. But when I walked in, before I could even put my books down, Willie was jumping all over me, Jelo was laughing and gurgling at me, and Mom was giving me kisses.

"Welcome home," she said, like I'd been on a trip or something.

"Hi, Mom." I took Jelo from her and held him up in the air in front of me. "Hi, bro," I said. I'd decided that instead of calling Jelo my half brother, I'd just call him half of brother—"bro." I jiggled him. "So, bro, how'd you like to go for a sleigh ride?"

"Great," my mom said. "I'll come too." As we bundled Jelo up in his snowsuit, she told me the same story that Josh had about Willie watching out for Jelo in the snow. "I heard that story already, Mom," I told her. What I wanted to say was, Why didn't you wait and let me take Jelo for his first sleigh ride? He's my half brother, not Josh's.

As we pulled and trudged through the snow, Willie jumped and ran ahead and Jelo laughed. That's when I realized that it was my last week with her before Christmas. "Oh dear," my mom said. "There's so much to do. I want this to be a special Christmas, especially because it's the first on the farm. It's your turn to spend Christmas Day with us, isn't it?"

Here's one of the most confusing things about having divorced parents: holidays. I alternate Thanksgiving and Easter. That means the year I spend Thanksgiving with my father, I have Easter with my mother, and vice versa. But Christmas gets broken into two parts. Like last year it was Christmas Eve with my mother and Christmas Day with my father. My friends think that I'm lucky because I get two whole Christmases that way, but mostly I get tired.

I bent over and brushed some gurgle spit off Jelo's chin. "Yup," I said. "You get Christmas Day."

"Oh, good," she said. "We'll open presents when you get here and then have a big feast. Let's start baking on the weekend. We'll invite George's parents. And of course Josh. Cynthia's already working on the menu." Mom threw a snowball at the side of the barn. "It'll be perfect. And the tree— we'll decorate it this weekend while you're still here."

"Mom," I said. "You forgot. I have a job. I should probably stay in town this weekend. Miriam and Dad need me to work Friday night and all day Saturday and Sunday. I told you on the phone."

"Oh." There was disappointment in her voice and all over her face. "Well, let's see what we can get done during the week. How about we make our wrapping paper after dinner tonight?"

"I've got so much homework."

"For a little while," she said, in a way that told me we would make wrapping paper no matter what.

So after George and Cynthia did the dishes and Mom put Jelo to bed and I got a start on my homework, my mother and I took over the kitchen to make wrapping paper the way we've done every Christmas since I was about three.

First we covered the table with a sheet of plastic. Next we filled old cups with water and lined them up in the middle of the table. Then we put a little food color in each of the cups. We make our paper with the white tissue wrapping paper they use in stores. The kind Miriam uses around clothes *inside* the box. Miriam would never use tissue paper on the outside—it's too thin and flimsy. Which is why it's just right for absorbing food color dyes.

My mother and I sat facing each other with the five cups of colored water between us.

"You do the first one," my mother said. I took four thicknesses of paper from my pile and folded them in half three times the long way. Then I folded triangles at each end. I ducked half the points I'd made in red dye and the other half in green dye.

"What kind of paper are you using at the store?" my mom asked as she dipped her first one.

"The best," I said. While we folded and dipped and laid our homemade batik wrapping paper out to dry, I described the gold shooting-star paper, the Santa heads on dark green, the red and green and gold checks, and all the great-looking ribbons.

Mom said, "We'll probably wrap all our presents for the price of one roll of their fancy paper. Plus we made it ourselves, so the wrapping on the present is like another gift."

She stopped folding and looked over at me.

"Which do you like better? The store paper or our paper?"

I didn't want to hurt her feelings, so I said, "Both I guess." But the truth was I was sick of making wrapping paper. My fingers were all stained with food color. I was tired and I still had a lot of homework to do. I also knew that when the paper dried and we unfolded it and used it to wrap, it would tear easily on the edges of boxes and be bulky where we folded it on the ends. And the colors dried into soft pastel shades—not Christmasy colors at all. Besides, I was going to wrap my presents at the store, so I'd be using Miriam's paper.

"How are you going to decorate the tree this year?" I asked.

She smiled and got that "I love Christmas" look in her eyes. "We'll use the same decorations we use every year, only we'll have the biggest tree ever. Remember those wonderful decorations you made when you were in grade school?"

I remembered the painted cookies—star, bell, tree, and Santa shapes with sparkles in different colors. "They're pretty ugly, Mom," I said. "Maybe you should start over. You know, since you moved and everything. I think you should get decorations all one color. Like, say, silver and white. It's very sophisticated."

"I like our old decorations, especially the ones you made. And I like an old-fashioned tree with lots of colors. In fact we're all making more ornaments this weekend." She looked me square in the eye. "I guess you'll have a one-color tree, with all

49

new things with your dad and Miriam. Which is fine for them. But we can't afford it and even if we could, I wouldn't want it."

I looked at the folded-up tissues, at my stained fingers, at the big old kitchen with worn linoleum floor, crooked cabinets, and cluttered counters. "I can't do this anymore," I said as I pushed my chair back and got up. "I've got to read *Romeo and Juliet* for Sister Bernard Marie's class."

My mother looked at me. I'd made her sad. But I was sad too. I knew I was being wicked to put down her Christmas ideas.

"I love *Romeo and Juliet*," she said. "Bring it down and read to me while I finish this job up."

"That's okay," I said.

I stood up and left the room without kissing her good night.

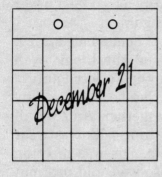

FIVE

4 Days Until Christmas

After school on Friday I went right to the mall, which gave me two hours to do *my* Christmas shopping before I went to work. Miriam paid me in advance for the weekend so I'd have plenty of money to do it.

This is what I got:

For Dad: A book, *Dress for Success,* so he'd know what to sell in his clothing store and what to wear when he was selling it.

For Miriam: One of those little hand vacuum cleaners, for picking up little piles of dust here and there, since she's so fussy about a clean house.

For Mom: A cookie jar shaped like a cow, since she's so into living on a farm and everything.

For George: A book, *Growing Your Own Food,* for the same reason.

For Cynthia: A book, *Your Country Kitchen Cookbook*.

For Jelo: A stuffed pink elephant that's soft and wonderful and just the kind I'd want if I were three months old.

For Josh: A dozen ballpoint pens, so he'd never have to borrow one from me again.

For George's parents: A jar of homemade apricot jam that says "homemade" on the label, even though I bought it at a store, the Perfect Pantry.

I didn't buy a present for Sue because we buy our presents for each other together. And we always get each other the same thing—like last year when we got identical wallets. She was meeting me at six during my break, so we could pick out our present for this year.

When I finished my shopping I took everything to Miriam's boutique. The store was hopping with customers, just the way it was every day before Christmas.

"Hi, Aviva," Miriam said as she led a customer to a pile of cashmere sweaters. "Am I ever glad to see you."

"Hi," I answered. "I did all my shopping."

"Great. Your table's waiting. A couple of customers said they'd come back when you were here to get their gifts wrapped." She smiled at her customer. "Aviva is our wrapper. She's terrific." She said it like she really meant it, not like she was trying to impress the customer with how great the people were who work in *her* store.

"Thanks," I said. Sometimes I like Miriam.

We finally closed up the store at nine o'clock. I was so tired that when I got in the back of the car to go home, I closed my eyes. Paper and ribbons and more paper and ribbons were jumbled in my mind. I was just about to drift off to sleep when I sat up with a start. "Aviva," Miriam was saying, "I was a little surprised at Sue tonight. I expected she'd at least thank us for inviting her to go to New York with you. I mean we are paying her way and everything. Don't you think that was rude, Roy?"

I leaned forward in the seat. I couldn't put off telling them any longer. "I didn't invite Sue," I said. "I mean, I decided not to. I asked Josh Greene. You said I could invite anyone I want."

"A boy?" Miriam had a sharp edge to her voice. "I thought it was understood you'd invite a girl."

"Josh is my friend. He's the most fun to be with. But don't tell any of my girlfriends because they'll get the wrong idea."

"You already asked him?" my dad said as he pulled the car into the driveway.

"Yeah. He's real excited. I mean Josh has had a horrible life. Bringing him is like an act of charity. He's never been on a plane or anything."

Miriam just sighed. I wondered if she'd already figured out that she wouldn't be sharing a hotel room with my dad.

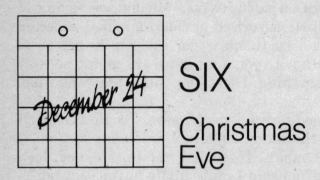

SIX

Christmas Eve

Monday was Christmas Eve, so we only kept the store open until three o'clock. It felt like Christmas, even though we were working. Miriam put out a tray of homemade cookies from the Perfect Pantry as a treat for the last-minute shoppers. People were saying Merry Christmas to one another and were already in a celebrating mood.

By one o'clock there were only a few customers and I had lots of time to wrap my presents. Miriam said that since Christmas shopping was almost over, I could use as many bows as I wanted. And I did. I was wrapping Jelo's present in Santa Claus paper when Miriam called from the front of the store, "Aviva, we have a customer who needs your help." I looked up. It was Josh.

He came over to my table. "I want to get a present for Jan," he explained. "Something special."

"What did you get George?" I asked as we walked around the store.

"Safety gloves to wear when he uses the chain saw. You know, to protect his hands," he said.

"That's nice and practical. Why don't you get my mother something practical too—like gardening gloves? There's a hardware store in the mall. They'll have—"

He interrupted me. "No. I want to get her something special. You know, nice."

"I got her a cookie jar that looks like a cow," I told him.

He scowled. "Something more personal." He pointed to a white silk and lace blouse hanging on a display hook. "Like that."

"Josh," I explained, "that blouse is pure silk. It costs seventy dollars."

When Miriam heard us talking about the blouse, she came over and offered to sell it to Josh for the wholesale price, which was thirty-five dollars. I still thought it was too much for him to spend and I didn't like it one bit that he got *my* mother a nicer present than I did.

While I wrapped his gift for him, I overheard him thanking Miriam and my dad for inviting him to come to New York City with them—like it was their idea or something.

When he came back to the wrapping table to get his package, he took a brown bag out of his pocket and put it on the table in front of me. "Jan sent these," he said. "We made them yesterday. We

55

made some for the tree, too. But you can't eat those. These are the eating kind."

I opened the bag and took out frosted bell-, star-, and tree-shaped cookies made with the same cookie cutters I'd used every year since I was a little kid.

"Thanks," I said. But I was thinking, I don't like Josh doing all the things I used to do with my mother, like I was dead or something.

This is how I spent the rest of Christmas Eve with Miriam and Dad: When we got home we all took naps. Then we spent a long time taking showers and getting dressed for dinner in a restaurant. Miriam helped me with my hair. She put some makeup on my eyes and cheeks. She's real good at that. When that was done, while I was still in my bathrobe, Miriam took me by the hand and led me into the living room.

"We have a present we want to give you right now," she said. "That one." Gorgeously wrapped gifts were piled under the Christmas tree. The box she was pointing to was wrapped in silver and white to match the decorations on the tree. Inside the box, wrapped in white tissue paper, was a red velvet dress with a white lace collar. The most beautiful dress I'd ever owned. Miriam said it was a classic and since I probably was finished growing I'd have it for years.

Dad said it looked beautiful on me and that I could go to the best places in New York City with my head held high.

We had a great time at dinner—like three adults. We talked about the store and how much money we made from the Christmas rush. Then we toasted Dad for being finished with teaching and starting his own business. But mostly we talked about New York and all the things we were going to do there.

When we got home we lit the vigil candles that Miriam had lined up on the windowsills and tabletops—at least two dozen of them. She put her favorite Christmas music on the tape deck and we sat under the Christmas tree and opened our presents. It was like a scene from her store window—Christmas magic.

Even though she said she loved it, I was sorry I hadn't gotten Miriam something more personal than a Dustbuster.

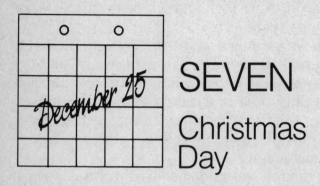

SEVEN
Christmas Day

My banana rang at eight o'clock the next morning. "Merry Christmas, darling." It was Mom. She was all excited about it being Christmas. I could hear voices, barking sounds, and Christmas music in the background. "Cynthia will pick you up in half an hour. We're all waiting for you, then we'll open our presents, so hurry."

I hung up my banana and lay back and moaned. I'd only had five hours' sleep and my stomach was upset from all the food and eggnog I'd had the night before. I sighed, jumped out of bed, washed, put on my new red dress, and tried to get back in the Christmas spirit.

At the farm everyone was still in their bathrobes or blue jeans, sitting around the kitchen table eating breakfast.

"Want some pancakes?" George asked from his position at the stove.

"No thanks," I said as my stomach turned over from the smell of fried bacon, melted butter, and hot maple syrup. "I'll just go put my presents under the tree."

My mother gave Jelo to Cynthia and came into the living room with me. As we stood in front of the tree, she put her arm around my shoulder and gave me a big hug. "What do you think of the tree?" she asked. "Isn't it incredible?"

"It's nice," I said.

It was a little lopsided, but it went all the way to the ceiling and was pretty in a homemade way. "There aren't any decorations on the lower branches," I said.

Mom laughed. "We couldn't keep Willie from playing and tugging on them. So everything has to be hung higher than he can reach." She started to unpack my shopping bags of perfectly wrapped, bow-covered gifts. "These will add a lot of color to the bottom of the tree." She smiled up at me. "They're beautiful, honey. You did a really good job. And just think, all over Burlington this morning people are unwrapping gifts that you made so beautiful."

I was the only one who was dressed up for present-opening, which is why I was named the one to pass out presents. I would rather have just sat there with Jelo on my lap, like Cynthia.

The presents I got were pretty weird. Mom and George gave me an I.O.U. poem. It was written on

a pretty card and wrapped in a box. But the poem
was like a riddle, so I didn't even know what the
present was that they owed me.

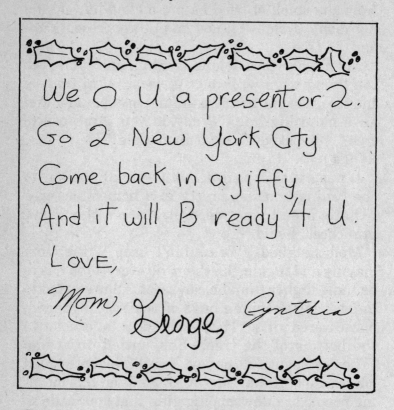

We O U a present or 2.
Go 2 New York City
Come back in a jiffy
And it will B ready 4 U.
Love,
Mom, George, Cynthia

I had a feeling that Josh had helped them write
the poem, which meant he knew what it was.
Which meant I could spend our three days in New
York City trying to get it out of him.

Besides the poem, Mom gave me a set of pretty
pink-and-white-striped sheets, which is a little pa-

thetic since my room is so grungy. I mean, new sheets won't help—they'll just make the room look worse.

Josh gave me a poem too. Another I.O.U. His was rolled up like a scroll and tied with a red ribbon.

ANIMALS COME and ANIMALS GO.
MY PRESENT FOR YOU ISN'T SO.
TURTLE TO BEGIN and DOG TO END.
MAKING SURE YOUR THINGS
DON'T FALL OR BEND.

"Thank you, I love it," I told them, even though I didn't know what I was thanking them for and whether I would love it or not.

My mom and George gave Josh a beautiful down jacket—one of the nicest I'd ever seen and certainly the best piece of clothing Josh Greene had ever had.

"It was George's idea," Mom told Josh as he tried it on. "But I picked out the blue-green color—to match your eyes."

Right then Josh's blue-green eyes were wet. I was probably the only one who noticed how he swallowed hard so tears wouldn't come out.

After presents George was going to bring Josh back to St. Joseph's Home so he could spend the rest of Christmas with Father Tierney and the other kids. I knew he'd rather stay at the farm with us, but he said, "I want to go back. You know, to help make it nice for the little kids."

Mom said, "Why don't you drive to town with them, Aviva?" She gave me a secret look that said, "Do it." I didn't go because of her look; I went because I wanted to tell Josh about some of the things Miriam and Dad said we'd do in New York.

I can't believe it, I thought, as we were getting into the car. We're flying out of Burlington airport tomorrow. I was glad that Josh had a nice jacket to wear. I also knew that Dad and Miriam were giving him a white shirt and tie, even though they didn't know him as well as Mom and George.

After we dropped Josh off and were heading back to the farm, George said, "Aviva, there's something I need to talk to you about." The way he said it made my stomach flip.

"What?" I asked.

"Well, Jan and I have been giving something a lot of thought and discussion. Now it's time to include you."

"What have you been talking about?" I was curious and scared at the same time.

"We've decided on something, but we won't do it unless we have your wholehearted approval. I don't want you to say yes or no today. After I ask you this question I want you to take at least a week to make your decision. Is that part understood?"

"Okay," I said. Maybe, I thought, they're admitting they made a mistake about moving to the farm and we can move back to town. I knew I could give them my yes vote on that one without thinking for another second.

George glanced at me nervously. "This is what it is. We would like to make arrangements for Josh to live with us—full-time. He needs a home and we have plenty of room. We all get along with him. As we see it, Josh is a wonderful kid who deserves a break. You know how much he loves to be with our family. The only thing we're not sure about is how it would affect you. Your mother's very concerned about that. We both are. And if you have any doubts, if you don't want it, things will go on as they have with Josh being a special friend of the family's, but still living at St. Joseph's Home."

Then he said what I'd wished he'd said about moving in with me and my mom, about having a baby, and about moving to the farm. "It's up to you. The deciding vote is yours."

"I know my answer," I said.

He put up his hand. "Don't tell me. Think about it for a week."

I already knew that my vote was no, no, no. Josh Greene should not move in with our family. And I knew for sure that I wasn't going to change my mind in a week, in a month, or in ten thousand years.

EIGHT

The Day After Christmas

The next morning Josh Greene and I sat side by side in seats 13B and 13D of a jet plane headed for New York City. I got the window seat for the take-off out of Burlington and he'd get it for the landing in New York. The deal was that going back to Burlington we'd do just the opposite.

Flying is just like I thought it would be, only scarier. Especially landing.

This is what Josh and I mostly said to each other as the cab drove us through the New York City streets to our hotel: "Look at that! Look!"

And my dad and Miriam kept saying, "Did you kids see that?"

But there is so much to see in New York City compared with downtown Burlington that I think it would take a lifetime to see it all. My dad said that if you ate in a different restaurant every night of the week, you would never get to all the restaurants because there would always be more new ones to try out. I loved the idea of eating your way through New York City, but Josh thought that if he found a restaurant he really liked, he'd want to go back to it instead of always trying out new ones.

We checked into the hotel and took the elevator to our rooms on the seventeenth floor. Miriam and Dad gave each other a sad look as Miriam headed through door 1703 with me and Dad headed through door 1704 with Josh.

The first thing Miriam did when we were alone in our room was open the drapes and look out the window. "Come here, Aviva," she said. I went over to the window. She put her arm around my shoulder. "Look. You can see all the way down Lexington Avenue. New York is a wonderful place," she said. "So vibrant. You'll have a wonderful time."

"I already am," I told her. And I was.

A few minutes later we were walking down Lexington Avenue on our way to lunch. This is what New York City is like: big, big, big and busy, busy, busy with people, people, people—all kinds of people—rushing, rushing, rushing. The weird thing is that with all those people they hardly look at one another. I guess that's because people know they aren't going to recognize anybody they see, except a famous person or something—which is why I looked at everybody.

"We want a table near the window," Miriam told the waiter at the restaurant she'd chosen for lunch. I made sure she got to sit next to Dad, which was the least I could do.

Dad, Josh, and I had hamburger platters and Miriam had a salad. She's afraid to gain weight. She says she has to look terrific in her own clothes or her business will suffer.

"Let's see what you guys are going to do today," Dad said as he ate the bacon that Miriam had taken out of her salad. I took out the little green plaid notebook I'd bought for the trip and opened to the schedule I'd figured out with Dad and Miriam. I'd written:

Day One In N.Y.C.

8:00 Fly to New York City
12:00 Eat lunch with Dad and Miriam.
1:30 + Ice skate and see tree
at Rockefeller Center.
+ Walk south on Fifth Ave
looking at Christmas
window displays.
+ Tour Empire State Building.
+ Take taxi back to hotel.
5:00 Meet Dad and Miriam
at hotel.
6:30 Dinner
8:00 Radio City Music Hall!

Between looking at the list of things we were going to do and looking out the window at all the people on the street, I was getting more and more excited. I mean, we were actually in New York City!

Dad moved our empty plates aside and put a street map on the table in front of us. "Now both of you pay attention," he said. We watched as he made little red arrows along the streets where we'd be walking and circled the sights we were to look for on the way, like St. Patrick's Cathedral and the windows of Saks Fifth Avenue.

Then he dug into his pocket and pulled out two envelopes. "Here," he said as he gave one of the envelopes to Josh and one to me. "This should be plenty of money for the next two days." He got real serious when he added, "Now I expect you two to watch out for each other." I was glad he didn't say something like, "Now, Josh, I'm depending on you to watch out for Aviva," like that's the way it should be because I was a girl and Josh was a boy.

After we split off from Miriam and Dad at the corner of Fifth Avenue and Forty-ninth Street, Josh said, "Do you really want to go ice-skating?"

"Of course," I said. "Don't you? Come on."

We walked toward Rockefeller Center. I kept my eye out for the Christmas tree, thinking I'd be able to see it around the tall buildings. But I couldn't.

"Look," Josh said as we rounded the corner. "There it is."

Chills went up and down my spine. It was the biggest, most beautiful tree I'd ever seen. With sparkling lights in all colors that shone even in the daytime.

We stood there staring at it. "It looks like the Christmas tree at the farm," Josh said.

"You must be kidding," I said. "This tree is three thousand times as big."

"But the lights are the same," he said.

I thought about how the Rockefeller Center tree would look if it were decorated in all silver or all gold like Miriam's trees and decided I liked it better just the way it was.

As we got closer to the tree, we came to a railing. We stood at it and looked down at the rink. Skaters wove in and out as they made big circles around the edge of the rink. There were hundreds of people standing at the railings watching the thirty or so people who were skating.

Josh said, "It's sort of silly, don't you think, to skate in front of people and everything. Let's skip it." That's when I thought, Josh Greene doesn't know how to ice-skate.

"Josh," I said. "Come on. I'm going to teach you how to ice-skate."

"I know how," he said.

I looked him right in the eye. "So let's go."

He didn't protest anymore and pretended like he knew how to skate. Which he did an hour later. We had to hold hands a lot in the beginning. I was glad we both had on thick gloves so it wasn't so much like *really* holding hands.

The thing I hadn't planned on during the trip to

New York was getting tired. By the time we'd skated, walked to the Empire State Building, gone to the top of the Empire State Building, and gotten back to the hotel, I was exhausted.

"Me too," Miriam agreed when we met in our room. "This is what we'll do. We'll each take a hot bath and climb in bed for thirty minutes. You'll be a new woman."

She was right. By six o'clock, when we met Dad and Josh in the hall, everyone looked perky and ready for a night on the town.

I'd never seen Josh in a shirt and tie. He looked pretty neat.

NINE

2 Days After Christmas

The next day was sunny. We all met for breakfast in the hotel coffee shop. After Dad, Josh, and I were served our eggs over easy with ham and Miriam her cold cereal with skim milk, my dad said, "Okay, guys, let's go over the schedule for today. You'll be on your own until five o'clock."

"That's cool," Josh said.

"No sweat, Dad," I said.

Half an hour later Josh and I were sitting in the back of a cab on the way to Battery Park to take a boat to the Statue of Liberty. In the afternoon we were going to the Metropolitan Museum of Art, where Josh said we'd see real Egyptian mummies.

This was the day of our trip I was most looking forward to. What I didn't understand was why

Josh was acting so nervous—fidgeting on his side of the backseat, not even looking out the window at all the city life we were passing.

When we'd paid the cabdriver and stood together ready to buy our ticket for the boat ride, I told him, "You're acting weird."

He looked up at the sky, then across the park at the big tour boat—anywhere but at me. "Aviva," he said, "I'm not going on that boat."

I couldn't believe it. First he doesn't tell me he can't skate when we make plans to go skating. Now he doesn't tell me he's afraid of boats or gets seasick or something when we plan a boat ride. "Why didn't you say something before?" I asked him. "We'd have planned to do something else." I looked around at the neighborhood—nothing but tall office buildings. "I mean, what are we going to do now?"

"You go," he said. "I'll meet you here when the ride's over."

"I'm not going to leave you here," I said. "We'll have to figure something out. New York's a big place. There must be something we can do." I was getting angrier as each second ticked by.

"Aviva, don't you get it? You're going to the Statue of Liberty alone. I have something I have to do."

"What are you talking about?"

"I'm going to see someone."

"Who?"

Instead of answering my question he said, "You'd better hurry up and get on the boat."

"Not unless you tell me who you're going to see."

"My father."

His father! I didn't know what question to ask first. "Where? Why? How?" I blurted out.

The horn on the boat tooted that it was time to leave the dock.

"I told you *who* I'm going to see. That's the only question I'm answering. Now get on that boat. Hurry up. I promise you I'll be here when you get back."

Josh's father. He'd deserted Josh after Josh's mother died and only showed up a few months ago when he heard that *his* mother—Josh's grandmother—was dead. Josh and I thought his father had come to say he was sorry and take care of Josh, but all he wanted was to see if his mother had left any money. Josh's father is a terrible man. And he was making Josh nervous and upset all over again.

"Look, Josh Greene, you'd better tell me what's going on, or I'm going to tell my father you left me alone all day."

"I knew it," he said as the tour boat tooted one last warning. "You'll ruin everything."

Josh gave the boat a last desperate glance as it pulled away from the shore. "And now you've gone and missed the boat. You're a spoiled, snitching brat, Aviva Granger."

I put my hands on my hips and stared right through his jerky blue-green eyes. "And you're nothing but a lying sneak who keeps secrets and doesn't trust anyone," I screamed.

I wanted to have a hitting, kicking, screeching fight like we used to have when we were little. I stamped my foot instead, which didn't even make a noise because I had on sneakers.

He stamped back. "You're still a spoiled brat," he said. But he didn't look angry anymore, just upset.

Maybe, I thought, if I stay calm and get him to talk about it, we can take the next boat to the statue. I decided to use psychology, like my mom does in an emergency. I pointed to a park bench near the water and said, "Let's sit down and talk about what's going on here."

He did what I said, which was a good sign. "Josh," I said in my best adult, calm tone, "how do you even know your father is in New York City?"

"I snuck into Father Tierney's office and read the stuff in my file," Josh said.

"And?"

"And I found a letter from a priest in New York City." He took a folded piece of paper from his down jacket pocket. "I copied down his name and address. It's where my father stays sometimes."

"What did the letter say?"

Josh looked over the water. "That he lives on the streets a lot. That he doesn't have a job or anything."

"He's a bum, Josh. He probably drinks too much and stuff like that. I don't think you should go see him. It'll make you sad."

Josh stared at me. His eyes were filled with a kind of anger I'd never seen before, even in our worst fights. "I hate him," he said. "He didn't take care of his own mother."

Or his own son, I thought. "So why do you want to see him?"

"To tell him how much I hate him," Josh said.

I decided that if I were Josh and I had a father like that, I'd want to do the same thing.

He stood up. "I answered your question. Now I'm going to get you a ticket for the next tour."

I stood up too. "I'm going with you to find your father."

"No you're not."

"Yes I am. My dad said we were supposed to watch out for each other. So there."

He sighed. Josh Greene knows when I'm not going to change my mind.

We used our Statue of Liberty money for a cab to St. Francis Residence. Every block we drove through was grungier than the one before. Poor-looking people walking around in a kind of daze. Others standing on corners or sitting huddled against the wind in doorways—just staring into space. One man tried to wash the cab window with a dirty rag.

"This is the Bowery," I told Josh. "Where a lot of homeless people live."

"And bums like my father," Josh added.

The first thing we saw at St. Francis Residence, even before we got out of the cab, was a line of about thirty men and women, mostly in ragged clothes, waiting at the ground-floor door. Would we have to get in the line in order to see the priest?

I looked around. "Let's go up the stairs and ring that bell," I suggested as I yanked on Josh's jacket to get him away from staring up and down the line of people—looking for his father.

I was beginning to hope that the priest could talk Josh out of telling his father how much he hated him, or at least set up a meeting between them in a civilized way. What I didn't want was for Josh or his father to lose their tempers. I figured it this way: If Thomas Greene could desert his own child and his own mother and not even care about them, he was capable of all kinds of cruelty—including physical cruelty.

Josh was still studying the line of people and looking up and down the street for his father, when a man opened the front door. "Hello," he said. "I'm Father Paulos." He was young—younger than my dad—and real tall, like a basketball player. "More helpers," he said in this cheery voice. "Come in, come in. Your friends are already in the soup kitchen setting up."

I started to say, "We're not . . ." when Josh elbowed me and blurted out, "Oh, the gang's here already. Terrific. Glad to help. I'm Josh, ah, Josh Campbell." Josh shook Father Paulos's hand.

"I'm Aviva," I said. What's Josh up to? I wondered. Why is he pretending?

As we followed Father Paulos down the stairs, Josh whispered to me, "Just act friendly, like you know everyone. This is the best way to find him."

Father Paulos turned toward us when we got to

the dark hall at the bottom of the stairs. "This your first time here?"

"Yes, Father," I said. That certainly was true.

"Fine," he said. "I'll put you in the back kitchen to make sandwiches and cut up vegetables."

He led us to the doorway of a big kitchen where about fifteen or so people—teenagers and adults—were doing just what he said we'd be doing. A tape deck played rock and roll and they were visiting with one another—laughing and stuff.

"Who serves the food?" Josh asked.

"The staff," Father answered. "Why? Do you want to help up front?"

"Yes," Josh said. "I'm doing a paper on the homeless for school." He's trying to find a way to get into the dining room to look for his father, I thought. "Homelessness is a terrible problem," Josh added.

Father Paulos was sad when he answered. "Yes, it is a terrible problem. And it gets worse every day. I don't have enough beds. Our homeless here take turns sleeping inside. There aren't enough beds for everyone."

Josh looked at the piles of food. "I thought that people who drink a lot of booze didn't eat so much," he said.

"You think the people on the streets are all alcoholics?" Father Paulos asked.

"'Course they're not, Josh," I said. "Some people are there for other reasons, like being crazy or something."

"Or just bad luck and no family to help," Father added. "And some are mentally ill. People who've been lost in the system. And even if the cause of their current situation is alcohol, what's the cause of that alcohol problem?"

We followed him into the kitchen. "If you want to meet some homeless people," he said, "why don't you cut up vegetables with Charlene over here." We stopped next to a young woman who was peeling carrots. "Charlene, meet Aviva and Josh. Show them the ropes."

Father Paulos moved off and Charlene smiled at us. "Hi," she said. She handed each of us a peeler, "Scrape away."

What did Father Paulos mean? I wondered as I scraped carrots and watched to see what Josh would do next. Did he mean that Charlene was homeless? While we cleaned and cut up about ten thousand carrots, Charlene told us her story.

"I got kids, you know," she started. "Younger than you—three of them. I had an apartment too, in Chicago. But then my husband picked up and left us. I couldn't get a job and take care of three little ones. Couldn't make enough money anyway, not to support my babies and pay the rent and a baby-sitter. Landlord evicted me. Put me right out on the street, furniture and everything.

"Stayed with my sister for a while. But she's only got two rooms and three kids of her own. Besides, with us there were just too many people in that little space. I knew her husband was going to leave her if we stayed another day and then she'd be as bad off as me. So here I am. I don't like to say I'm homeless, just that I'm in between homes. You know, so it doesn't sound so bad."

She stopped scraping and looked at me—big sad, tired brown eyes that were filling up with tears. "But it is. It's real bad."

Josh stopped working and looked around the large kitchen. "Where are your kids now?" he asked.

"I wouldn't let them live on the streets, not my kids." She took a photo out of the pocket of her shirt and showed us three kids in a row in front of a small Christmas tree. The oldest held the youngest on her lap, like me and Jelo.

Charlene pointed to the girl. "That's Crissy, my oldest. She's still with my sister. Just 'cause she helps out some." She pointed to the baby and a boy who looked about four years old. "Todd and Gina are in foster homes—but just until I find a place. Get myself straightened out. But what kind of job can I get that's going to give me enough money to start over? What am I going to do?"

She sighed. So did I. I didn't have any ideas on what could make her life better.

A man walked by with a kettle of steamy soup in each hand. "I'll help," Josh said as he reached out and took one of the kettles.

"Great," the man said as he let go of half his load. "Thanks."

"Be right back," Josh said to me.

But he wasn't. Charlene and I had added piles of peeled and cut potatoes to our piles of carrots before Josh came back.

"What took you so long?" I asked. "Did you see him?"

He whispered in my ear, "Come on, we're leaving." By the way he said it, I knew it wasn't because we were rushing off to see the mummies at the Metropolitan Museum of Art.

"What's the hurry?" I asked as we went out the basement door. "We didn't even say good-bye to Father Paulos." We were back in the cold air outside the Residence. "What happened? Did you see him?" I asked. "Josh, what did you do?"

"I didn't do anything," he said. "I talked to some of the men in the dining room. Come on. We have to hurry before he leaves." His eyes were filled with excitement and determination, like when we have a tie score in basketball and there's only a few seconds left on the clock. He started to run. I followed.

As we jogged two blocks uptown and one block east, Josh explained. "This guy that knows him said Tom Greene hangs out near Larry's Bar and Grill."

When we reached the bar we looked through the greasy front window. There were lots of bummy guys, but none of them was Josh's father.

"He's not here," I said.

Josh stepped back from the window and looked up and down the street. I could barely hear him when he said, "There he is."

I looked in the direction of Josh's angry gaze. Sleeping in a doorway, huddled against the cold in a thin sports jacket, was Thomas Greene—first-class bum and horrible father.

I put my hand on Josh's arm. Even through the down jacket I could feel how tense he'd become. "Be careful, Josh," I said. "Don't get hurt."

I felt my heart pounding inside my chest as I followed Josh to the doorway and his sleeping father. Josh swung his leg back. Oh no, I thought, he's going to kick him. But he didn't. He just nudged him with his foot.

Thomas looked up at us through half-closed, blurry eyes and slurred, "How about a quarter for a cup of coffee?"

"I hate you," Josh screamed. "I hate you." His voice quivered.

"Then leave me alone." Thomas's face turned from half-asleep drunk into angry drunk when he shouted, "Or I'll beat you up." He threw his empty whiskey bottle at us.

I jumped to get out of the way.

Josh swung his leg back like he was really going to kick him—hard.

I pulled Josh back. "Don't." I moved in front of him so he'd have to look at me and tried the best way I knew to get him to be reasonable. "I'm scared, Josh," I said. "Let's get out of here before something awful happens. He doesn't even know who you are."

It worked. "I wouldn't waste the energy beating him up," Josh said as he turned away. "Even though he deserves it."

On the way back uptown in the cab Josh stared at the back of the driver's head—not once looking out the window or at me. "Josh," I said, "he didn't know who you were. Being drunk like that all the time is a disease. He's a sick, mean man. Just forget about him."

Josh finally turned toward me. "What do you think I'm trying to do?" he said.

"Here's something else to think about," I said. "What are we going to say to Miriam and my dad about what we did today? I mean about the Statue of Liberty and the Museum."

The corners of his mouth turned up in a sad smile. "We'll tell them what a great, interesting time we had," he said.

At dinner Miriam said, "So, guys, tell us all about the Statue of Liberty."

"It's bigger than I thought it would be," Josh said.

"Did you see the engraving of the poem that was written for the Statue?" my dad asked. Then he started reciting, "'Give me your tired, your poor, your huddled masses yearning to breathe free.'"

"The neighborhood around that park where the boats go from has a lot of the homeless people," I said.

"Lots of 'your tired, your poor' and 'your huddled masses' there," Josh added. "What I wonder is, what does Liberty do for them?"

"Well, let's not think about sad things now," Miriam said. "How about the Metropolitan Museum of Art. What was that like?" She smiled at Josh. "Did you see the mummy you were looking for?"

"Yes," Josh said. "He was wrapped in rags. Not much life left in those rags."

Josh is still thinking about his father, I thought.

After dinner we walked back to our hotel, looking in store windows along the way. There must be a lot of rich people in New York City, I thought, to afford a pocketbook that costs three hundred dollars or a pair of boots that costs five hundred dollars. "I would love a pair of those boots," Miriam said as she looked longingly through the glass at a pair of black leather boots with silver studs up the back.

Dad put his arm around her shoulder. "Why don't you get them?" he said. "Tomorrow. Your store is going gangbusters. I say you get them."

She grinned up at him, all happy and excited. "You're right. I'm going to get them."

As we moved away from the store window, Miriam grabbed my arm. "Watch out," she said. I looked in the direction she was pulling me away from. There, next to the store with five-hundred-dollar boots and three-hundred-dollar pocketbooks was a woman wrapped up in a dirty blanket trying to stay warm by the heat coming up from the subway grating. She didn't ask us for money or anything. Didn't even move. She could be dead, I thought, as we turned away from her, and we wouldn't even know.

We continued up Fifth Avenue, past the glittery, expensive stores, and I wondered about that woman and how she ended up sleeping on the streets. When did she start being that way? Where was her family? Her parents? Were they all dead? Had she ever been married? Did she have children somewhere? Would Charlene end up like that?

"Penny for your thoughts," Miriam said as we were getting into bed.

"I was just thinking about that lady next to the shoe store," I said. "That's all."

"Oh, don't," Miriam said, in a disgusted tone. "She doesn't have anything to do with you. She's just another drunk. The city really should do something about it. They shouldn't let them stay on Fifth Avenue. They should keep them on the Bowery where they belong. It used to be you didn't see things like that in this part of the city." She reached over to turn off the light. "I hope she didn't ruin the evening for you, Aviva. I want everything to be perfect for you on this trip."

I lay back in the darkness and thought, Miriam's magic. Magic Christmas. Magic trip. Magic life. Well, Miriam, sometimes things can't be perfect. Sometimes there isn't enough magic to go around.

TEN

3 Days After Christmas

I woke up to a loud knock on our hotel room door. "Aviva, Miriam, wake up," my father was calling through the door. I opened it. "Have you seen Josh?" he asked.

"No," I said, half asleep. "What time is it?"

"Seven," he said. "Josh isn't in his bed. I checked the coffee shop. He's not there either."

Miriam was awake now and sitting up in bed. "You probably just missed each other in the elevator or something," she said. "He'll show up at breakfast." She leaned over and looked at her travel alarm clock. "He knows we meet for breakfast at eight. Are you going to pack before we leave for the showrooms? I think we'd better check out so we don't have to come back to the hotel at lunchtime. I have a feeling . . ."

My father wasn't paying any attention to her. "What do you think, Aviva?" he asked me. "Do you have any idea where Josh could be? He has his jacket."

"Well, that's it," Miriam said. "He went for a walk. Probably wanted to act big—you know, be on his own. I think Josh can take care of himself, don't you, Aviva?"

"Did he leave a note?" I asked my father.

"I don't think so. But I'll check again."

"Me too," I said. I tried to keep the panic out of my voice. The panic inside me that was screaming that Josh Greene might be out looking for his father to tell him—maybe even show him—how much he hated him. And then what would Thomas Greene do to his son?

As my dad and I headed out the door, Miriam called, "Roy, honey, wear your navy suit today. These are the top design rooms we're going to. Maybe with the striped maroon tie. . . ." Dad closed the door to Room 1703 and opened the door to Room 1704. Please be in here, Josh, I prayed. But he wasn't and there wasn't a note either.

At eight-fifteen he still hadn't shown up for breakfast. Miriam was getting angry. "You should have brought Sue," she said to me. "At least she's reliable. I wouldn't be surprised if that boy isn't damaged with the hard life he's had. He'll always mess things up for himself." She looked at her watch. "He's going to make you late for your city bus tour, Aviva."

"Dad," I said in a low voice. "I think I might

know where Josh went." Then I told them about Josh finding his father and hating him and how scared I was that Josh's father would hurt him. By the end of the story I was crying.

Miriam was furious at me. "How could you lie to us like that, Aviva. Telling us you were one place when you were someplace else? You've been as irresponsible as Josh."

My dad glared at Miriam. "Leave her alone." She glared back at him as if it were his fault. "Now what are we going to do?" she said.

"I'll take care of it." He pushed his chair back and stood up. "Come on, Aviva," he said. "We're going to find Josh."

"What about the showroom appointments?" Miriam asked.

"You go on alone," my father said. "We'll meet you back here at three o'clock. If things get straightened out before then, I'll catch up with you at the showrooms or at lunch."

He didn't kiss her good-bye or anything.

First we had the cab take us to St. Francis Residence, but Father Paulos said he hadn't seen Josh or his father. "It would be better for the boy," Father Paulos concluded, "if he didn't have anything to do with his father. I'll keep in touch with Father Tierney if there's any change in that." He shook my father's hand. "I'm sure you'll find the boy, but check back here if you run into any trouble." When he said good-bye to me he gave me a funny smile that was like a scolding for deceiving him the day before.

We had the cabdriver go slowly up and down the streets around St. Francis Residence. After about ten minutes I shouted, "There he is. On the corner. That's him." I pointed to two men standing on the corner, and the cab pulled over to the curb. "With that other man."

"You stay here," my father said. "I'll take care of this."

He got out of the cab and so did I. "I'm coming with you," I told him.

When we got to the corner I heard Josh's father say to the other man, "It's all feathers. Ten dollars it's yours." He held out Josh's blue down jacket. He was actually selling it.

"Where's Josh?" I screamed. "What did you do to him?"

My dad grabbed my arm. "Get back in the cab," he ordered in his strongest father voice. I stepped back a few steps toward the cab while my dad went up to Thomas Greene and talked to him in a quiet, calm voice. In my head I saw Josh lying in a doorway, cut up with a broken whiskey bottle, a big red gash on his forehead. Or maybe beaten to death.

A minute later my dad was next to me, leading me to the cab. Josh's jacket was tucked under his arm. "It's okay," he said. "He's seen Josh and no one's hurt anyone. As far as I can tell, Josh just hung out with him and then gave him the jacket. He says Josh's in the park."

"Dead in the park," I shouted.

"Calm down," Dad said.

"Did he even know who Josh was?" I asked.

"He knew," my dad said in a sad voice. "You're right about him. He's a cold man."

"What about the jacket?" My voice was shaking.

"I bought it from him for fifteen dollars," my dad said.

"He stole that jacket from Josh," I screamed. "And probably hurt him or something." I pulled away from my dad to go after Thomas Greene, but he'd disappeared.

My father put his arm around my shoulder. "You calm down right now. We're going to find Josh and he'll be okay. Do you understand me?"

I took a deep breath. He was right. Being hysterical wouldn't do anyone any good, particularly Josh. But I still wasn't convinced we'd find him. Or if we did that he'd be all right.

The cab took us to a little park—a regular hangout for homeless people. When we got out I spotted Josh, sitting alone on a park bench. "You stay here, Aviva," my dad said. "I'll get him."

"No," I said in a firm, calm voice. "I'll get him. I know Josh Greene better than you, or anyone. I can talk to him."

This is what surprised me: My father said, "Okay. I'll wait here."

I put Josh's jacket under my arm and walked past the benches dotted with homeless people and their bags and carts filled with their belongings.

When I reached Josh I sat down next to him. He looked awful—tired, sad, and cold.

"Josh," I said, "what are you doing here?"

"Leave me alone," he answered. "Go away."

"I'm not going anywhere until you tell me what's going on."

He didn't answer.

I didn't budge.

Finally he said, "I'm staying with my father."

"Why?"

"I'm going to help him."

Had Josh gone crazy? I wondered. Did his father drug him or something? "I don't understand," I said. "You hate him."

"He told me," Josh said. "Last night he told me."

"Told you what?"

"Why he drinks like that. Why he left."

"Why?"

Josh looked right at me. "When my mother died he felt like she abandoned him. He was so sad that he ran away. He couldn't help it."

"That's what he told you?"

"Yes," he said. "And then I remembered."

"What?"

He didn't answer.

"What did you remember?"

He stared at a spot on the pavement in front of his shoes and spoke in a rough-sounding whisper. "I remember being in a crib. A yellow crib. And he was on the couch. I was real little. But I could stand. I was standing at the rail of the crib. Crying. I must have fallen asleep or something because when I woke up he wasn't there. After a while I stopped crying because it didn't make any difference. I was cold and hungry. No one came."

"And then what happened?"

"Nothing. I don't remember anymore. I guess my grandmother found me. But I remember that feeling of being cold and deserted."

"Right. And that's why you hate him," I said. "So why would you want to stay here with him?"

"Because I know now that's how he felt when my mother died. Deserted. Maybe that's why he did it to me. If I leave, I'm doing it to him. He's my father. I have to take care of him. This is where I belong."

"Josh, that's crazy," I said. "He might have been just as bad *before* she died. He probably was." My dad was coming toward us. I put up my hand to stop him and turned back to Josh. "Listen to me, Josh. Your father was a grown-up and he deserted a baby. This is different." I bent my head down so he'd have to look at me. I held out his jacket. "Josh, he was selling the jacket that George gave you for ten dollars to buy liquor. He isn't a father to you. He never has been."

"I'm staying."

"And deserting us. That's what you'll be doing."

"What do you mean?"

"What about George and my mom and Jelo?"

"So?" he said. "They're your family. You're related. They're your flesh and blood. And he's my flesh and blood."

"George isn't my flesh and blood," I said. "But it's like we're related. It's the same way with you and us. I mean you're always around."

Josh didn't say anything.

This is when I changed my mind about something that I said I'd never change my mind about in a thousand years.

"Josh," I said. "George and Mom and I want you to live with us all the time. Now that we have the farm, there's plenty of room. George loves having a grown-up son-type person around."

He still didn't say anything. Finally he took the jacket from me and put it on. "He was really selling my jacket?"

"The only way my dad could get it from him was to pay him fifteen dollars. Father Paulos even said that you should stay away from him. That he's no good for you."

"You don't think I can help him?"

"Maybe someday. Father Paulos will let you know if there's any change. But right now, Josh Greene, you've got to help yourself. You're just a kid."

I knew he was still hesitating in his heart. "Remember, he didn't pay attention to a crying baby. He left you alone in that crib. You were helpless. What kind of person would do that? I don't care how drunk or sick he was. I mean, imagine if it were Jelo."

I looked him straight in the eye. He had the look of that little baby, alone in the crib.

"Josh," I said. "Let's go home."

As we walked toward my dad, Josh said in an almost normal Josh-voice, "Aviva Granger, swear on your life you won't tell anybody the stuff I told you."

I looked at him. "What?" I said. "What did you tell me?"

He smiled. "Good," he said. "And don't say anything about that I might live on the farm. I want to think about it."

That's what I couldn't believe. I thought he'd jump at the opportunity to move in with us.

"You okay?" my dad asked Josh when we reached him at the edge of the park.

Josh stood his tallest when he answered, "Yes, sir. I'm fine. I'm sorry I caused any trouble."

"Josh," my dad said. "It wasn't trouble. I was worried about you." My dad had tears in his eyes. "I'm so relieved you're all right, son," he said. And he put his arm around Josh's shoulder and gave him a hug.

I thought, The next thing you know my dad will want Josh to live with *him* too. And Josh will go back and forth like me. Would we have the same schedule or do opposite weeks, Josh being on the farm while I'm with Dad and Miriam and then the other way around? When I remembered Miriam I knew there was no way Dad would be able to have Josh living with him.

The cab dropped Josh and me off at the hotel, and Dad went on to meet Miriam at the restaurant where they were scheduled to have a business lunch.

This is what Josh ate for lunch in the hotel coffee shop: vegetable soup, fried chicken platter, a basket of rolls, a milk shake, and a piece of cheesecake. I was real glad he was having lunch with me instead of picking through garbage pails looking for scraps.

The whole way back to Burlington Miriam hardly spoke to Josh. When we dropped him off at St. Joseph's Home, Dad said, "I'll go in with Josh." To tell Father Tierney what happened, I thought.

"Thank you," Josh said to Miriam as he got out of the car. "It was a great trip."

"You're welcome, Josh." She said it like Josh was a customer who had spent hours trying on everything in her store and didn't buy anything.

As Dad and Josh were going into St. Joseph's, Miriam turned around from the front seat and said, "Well, Aviva, I hope you've learned your lesson. You can't be too careful about who you choose for friends."

"Josh is still my friend," I told her. "He's my best friend." Then I added, "But I think you're a snob."

When my dad got back in the car he must have noticed that Miriam and I weren't talking to each other. And she didn't say anything when he said, "Josh Greene is one very special kid, Aviva. You're lucky to have him for a friend."

Driving along the dark, icy road in the moonlight, I realized how glad I was to be back in Vermont and glad to be going home, even if it wasn't my old house on Elm Street. When we pulled up in front of the house, Miriam said, "What a nice big place. So pretty in this snowy landscape with the old-fashioned Christmas tree in the window. It's so quaint. This must be wonderful for Willie, so much space to run around in."

Dad said, "Not now, Miriam," like he was scolding her.

When I got out of the car, I thought, They are going to have one major fight. And it's going to be partly about my dog. I already knew that joint custody wasn't so good for Willie and it was better for him to stay on the farm. But I wasn't ready to tell Miriam that she'd never have to worry about having my dog in her apartment again.

I gave my dad a big thank-you kiss. As I went to the front door, I could see my mom and George on the living room couch watching the seven o'clock news. Jelo was in the middle of the room going back and forth in his house swing. Willie was lying on the rug trying to decide which to watch—Jelo moving in the swing or the images moving on the TV screen. The front door was unlocked so I just walked in. I could hear Cynthia preparing dinner in the kitchen.

When I yelled, "I'm home," they all came running, except Jelo of course. I got lots of hugs and kisses. It was the first time I gave George a hug because I wanted to and not because I had to. I couldn't get over how excited they were to see me. Jelo was jumping up and down so hard in his swing, I thought it would topple over. I took him out and gave him a big hug and kisses all over his soft little face.

"Well, Aviva, we sure missed you," my mom said.

"But you've kept us very busy in your absence," George added.

"Let's show her now," Cynthia said.

"Or should we make her wait until after dinner?" my mom asked.

"My Christmas present," I screamed. "I think I should get it right now."

"If you say so," my mom said. "Let's bring your suitcase upstairs and then you can have it." I saw her wink at Cynthia.

George picked up my suitcase. Mom took my coat. And Cynthia said, "I'll carry Jelo."

When we got upstairs the first thing I noticed was a sign on my door:

> *Welcome Home, Aviva!*
> *Merry Christmas!*

I opened the door. "Oh," I yelled. "Oh, oh, oh! It's beautiful."

They'd given my room a make-over. No more hundred-year-old wallpaper. The walls were now a beautiful shade of peach. And instead of torn shades there were white lace curtains in the windows. The new sheets were on my bed, covered by a big puffy flowered quilt. And on the floor was George's old puke green rug that he'd had for about a thousand years. Actually it didn't look so pukey with the peach walls. Over the bed was my favorite rainbow poster, like always, only now it was in a neat black frame.

"It's beautiful," I said again. They all talked at once, saying who did what and did I like this and did I like that. There was even a pillow for my desk chair that matched the sheets on the bed. "It's perfect," I said. And it was.

During dinner they asked me all sorts of questions about New York and the trip. I told them all I could without telling them about Josh and his father. The more I talked about the trip the happier I was to be home.

What I kept wondering was should I tell my mom and George my decision about Josh living with us or wait for them to ask.

Later when Mom and I were doing the dishes, she said, "I hope you don't mind that we picked out so many of your things. We were just going to paint, but once we got started, we got carried away."

"I love it, Mom," I said. I didn't tell her I was thinking about Charlene's kids, who couldn't even live with *their* mom. Or Josh, whose father would sell his own son's jacket. Then without even thinking about it, I said, "I told Josh we want him to move in with us."

She turned the water off and faced me. "Are you sure?" she asked.

"Whether I am or not," I said, "it's too late. I already asked him."

"Are you sorry you did?" she said.

"No," I answered. "I'm not."

We were both quiet for a minute, thinking about what it would be like to have Josh in our house all the time. Mom turned the water back on, rinsed a plate, and handed it to me.

"You know what I think?" I said as I took the plate.

"What?"

"I think there's plenty of love in this house to go around."

The next day was Saturday. Almost as soon as he got up, George went to St. Joseph's Home to talk to Father Tierney and Josh.

It was lunchtime when George drove into our drive—alone.

"I guess Josh decided no," I said as we waited for George to come in.

"We'll see," my mother said.

When George came into the kitchen he was smiling, but it was a smile with a little sadness in it.

"Well?" my mom asked.

"Well," George answered. "Our girl, Aviva here, had herself a pretty exciting time in New York City. I'll say this for you, Aviva"—he put his hand on my shoulder and gave it a little squeeze— "you're a loyal friend not to have told us what happened."

My mom looked at me. She looked scared. "What happened?" she asked. "What didn't you tell us?"

George told her the whole story about our looking for Thomas Greene and Josh staying out all night and his father trying to sell his son's jacket. I knew that Josh hadn't told him the part about remembering being left in the yellow crib. And neither did I.

"Is he moving in?" Mom asked when George had finished the story about our trip.

George smiled. "Yes," he said. "On New Year's Eve."

"Hooray," my mother yelled. "That's perfect. New beginnings."

The beginning of what? I wondered.

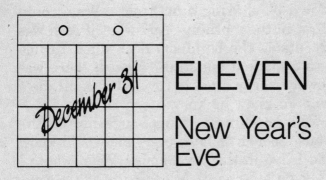

ELEVEN

New Year's Eve

Over the next two days we turned the spare bedroom into Josh's room. It didn't have old wallpaper, which made it easier to paint. Cynthia and I did that—in white. My mother made curtains out of navy-and-red-striped sheets to match the ones she bought for the bed. George got a secondhand bureau and painted it dark blue. The neatest thing— the thing I would have loved—was that they made a desk for him out of two red file cabinets and an old flat wooden door.

When I picked out my room when we moved in, I turned down the one Josh was getting. As I looked it over now, ready for Josh's arrival, I wondered if I had made a mistake. It was a smaller room than mine, but it was in the back of the house and had a beautiful view of the barn and fields. I knew that if

Josh was choosing between my room and his, this would be his choice.

The night before Josh moved in with us I lay awake going over all the things I hadn't thought about when I first asked him.

#1. We'd be sharing a bathroom. Who would use it first in the morning? And what if Josh was waiting outside the bathroom door when I came out and I'd made a big stink? Even if there was that flowery spray stuff to cover the smell, he'd know and I'd know he knew.

#2. We'd be going to school together on the school bus. Sooner or later everyone would know Josh and I live in the same house. What would I tell the kids at school? My friends are always thinking Josh and I are boyfriend and girlfriend instead of just friends. They'll drive me crazy about this when they hear.

#3. Josh will be at the farm all the time and I will be there only half the time. What about when I'm at Dad's? In the next four years Josh will be living with my mother as much time as I've lived with her since first grade.

The biggest question was, What if I'd made a mistake saying that Josh could live with us? I hated being the one responsible. One thing was for sure, I was glad that no one asked my opinion about whether Mom should marry George and have Jelo, because I know I would have voted N-O. And the truth was, living with George was working out okay and I loved having a baby half brother. But did I really want to have a sort-of-orphan best friend living in my house as a sort-of-brother? Well, I thought, if it doesn't work out, it will be my own fault for saying yes.

On New Year's Eve morning I looked awful. There were dark circles under my eyes. I watched from behind my lace curtains as Josh and Father Tierney got out of the St. Joseph's Home van. Father carried Josh's suitcase and Josh carried a duffel bag. His whole life, I thought, in two pieces of luggage.

I heard the front door open and close. I went into the hall and listened. Mom and George and Willie were making a big fuss over Josh. Then Father Tierney said he'd love to see Josh's room in his new home.

I ran back to my room and closed the door. But I didn't want it to look like I was hiding or something, so I got Myrtle from her sunny spot near my bureau, put her in her house, and carried it down the hall.

"Hi," I said to Josh when we met outside his room.

"Hi," he said back.

I put Myrtle's box down next to Josh's desk. "Myrtle might as well stay in your room," I said.

"Good idea," my mother said to me. To Josh she said, "I'd forgotten all about Myrtle and that wonderful home you and George made for her."

Josh didn't say anything. The fact is that Josh Greene didn't look very happy for someone who'd just been given a home after living like an orphan.

He had circles under his eyes even bigger than mine.

All the adults were in a great mood, talking about Josh's new room and the great view. Josh sat on the edge of the bed and listened to them talking and laughing. No one but me seemed to care that Josh was acting depressed.

"Would you like to stay for lunch, Jim?" George asked Father Tierney.

"Gotta get back," he said.

I wondered if Josh was sad because he was going to miss Father Tierney and the other kids at the Home.

"Well, then," my mother said, "why don't we give Josh time to unpack." She put her hand on his shoulder. "Lunch will be in half an hour, dear."

"I'm not hungry," Josh said. "Thank you. I've got some things I have to do."

"Then you go do them," George said. "Maybe tomorrow we'll look at that chicken coop, see what we can figure out."

Josh's eyes lit up for a second. "Yeah?" he said.

"I got a book out of the library on how to raise them free-range, natural."

"Great!" Josh said.

I thought the first day Josh was part of our family was going to be fun. I thought we'd go sledding or take Jelo for a sleigh ride or even go ice-skating. George had some old skates he said would fit Josh and we'd shovel off the pond.

Instead, Mom and Cynthia went grocery shopping for our special New Year's Eve dinner. George worked on a story he was doing for the paper. I baby-sat for Jelo. And Josh Greene stayed in his room the whole day.

As I fed Jelo his applesauce I thought, Why should anyone look forward to welcoming in another year of days like this, especially if a boring, depressed boy-your-age was about to share the rest of your life as a sort-of-brother?

Things picked up a little when Mom and Cynthia got back with the groceries. We put some rock and roll on the radio and started working on the preparations for our New Year's Eve dinner party. Besides the food, they'd gotten party hats and horns. While Cynthia and Mom started making the food, I made up a menu for the middle of the table—like in a New York City restaurant.

As I drew a ribbon at the top of the menu, I thought, Josh should be doing this, especially since he's not cooking anything and he's a much better artist than I am. He could probably even turn the list of courses into a poem or riddle.

What was weird was that no one said anything about Josh being in his room all day. When Cynthia left the kitchen to change her clothes I said to Mom, "You'd think Josh would be a little more excited or something. I mean isn't he glad he moved here?"

"It's a big change for him," my mother said, as she handed me the mozzarella cheese to chop up for the manicotti stuffing.

New Year's Eve Dinner
at
CHEZ JELO !

Antipasto à la George

Aviva's Salad

Manicotti à la Mom

Breads by Cynthia

Killer Chocolate Cake

At midnight the diners will

ring in the New Year, being

careful not to wake up Jelo.

"Do you think he feels guilty about leaving the other kids at the Home?" I asked.

"That's part of it, I'm sure." Mom poured herself a cup of coffee, sat down, and watched me work. "I think he's a little scared too," she said.

"Scared?"

"Scared to trust anyone to really care and not desert him," she said. I still didn't tell her about how awful it was when he was a baby in the crib. She went on. "First his mother died, then his father left him, then his grandmother died. And now all he has is Father Tierney and us. So, he's scared. Scared to trust that anyone will really take care of him."

"He also feels guilty about leaving his father on the street," I added.

"That too."

I'd stopped chopping and we looked at each other. We were getting pretty depressed ourselves. "Is he going to be this way all the time?" I asked.

My mother smiled. "Of course not," she said. "But it will take a while for him to adjust."

"It's weird," I said. "He seems like a different person. I mean now that I know he's living here."

"Give it time," my mother said.

Once or twice during the afternoon George went into Josh's room, but Josh never came out. And George never talked to us about why Josh wasn't coming out. All he'd say was, "Let him be. He has something to do."

When I went to the bathroom to take my shower, I ran down the hall, so if Josh opened his door he wouldn't see me in my raggy yellow bathrobe. Did he wonder why I was running? Did he look through the keyhole?

Later, when I was all dressed for dinner, I stopped at his door and listened. Was Josh crying? I put my ear up to the door. The sounds I heard weren't crying. It was more of a scraping sound, like scratching wood with a knife. I thought, Josh is probably writing graffiti in his wooden desktop. I wondered what it would say. Would I sneak in his room sometime when he was outdoors with George and look? Would he sneak in my room when I was at my dad's and poke through my things?

When I went back into the kitchen, my mother said, "Aviva, that blue sweater looks real pretty with your dark hair, but why the long face? Are you still worried about Josh?"

"It's giving me the creeps," I said, "the way he stays in his room." I didn't tell her that I thought he was carving all over the nice desk that we'd given him.

"Well, it's time he showed his face," she said. "You go tell him that dinner will be in an hour and he should help you set the table."

"Me?"

"You."

I knocked on the door and called his name. Would he say, "Come in"? Was that something we'd do, go into one another's rooms?

"Who is it?" he called back through the closed door.

"Who do you think it is?" I was getting cross. Didn't he even know what my voice sounded like?

"Don't come in," he yelled, sort of panicky. "What do you want?"

Was he half-dressed? Should we put locks on our doors for privacy?

"Dinner's in an hour," I shouted through the door. "My mother said you should help set the table."

"Okay," he answered. "I'll be there in half an hour."

Maybe he wants time to shower and everything, I thought as I went back downstairs. Or to carve up some more of our furniture!

I started to set the table by myself and listened to hear if he'd use the shower, but he didn't. What about the seating arrangement at the table? Where would Josh sit? Our table is a circle and everyone has regular places. Going clockwise, it was Mom, me, Cynthia, George. When Jelo is big enough for a high chair, I figure he'll go between Mom and George. But what about Josh? I hoped he'd sit between Cynthia and George and keep me out of it.

Finally, at seven-thirty—eight hours and ten minutes after he'd moved into our house—Josh Greene left his bedroom and came downstairs. I didn't even look up but kept moving around the table, putting down knives and forks.

I knew Josh was standing in the doorway. "Merry Christmas," he said.

I looked up. He was smiling and looked pretty much like the Josh Greene I sat next to in school since first grade.

"It's New Year's Eve," I said. "Did you lose track of time locked up in your room?"

He walked over to me, his hands behind his back.

"Merry Christmas," he said again. He held out two blocks of wood, one in each hand. "Here's your present."

They were bookends. Bookends carved out of wood.

"My present?" I said as I took them from him. One bookend had a handcarved dog sitting with his back to where the books go, the other had a turtle with her belly facing the direction of the books. Willie and Myrtle. They weren't painted or anything. They just had the natural look of the wood showing the knife marks and waxed to a glow. "You made these?"

"Sure," he said. "Remember?" He chanted the poem he had given me Christmas morning.

"Animals come and animals go.
My present for you isn't so.
Turtle to begin and dog to end.   •
Making sure your things don't fall or bend."

I put the bookends side by side in the middle of the table, like a centerpiece, and leaned the menu against them. "They're beautiful, Josh. I love them."

He picked up the menu. "I like your menu too."

"Well," I said, "it's not a poem or anything."

"But it's pretty." He put it back, picked up the silverware, and continued laying it out where I'd left off. I was still admiring the bookends and thinking that families are like bookends—they hold you up. "This is what you were doing in your room all day?" I asked Josh. "Making my present?"

He gave me his broadest, most mischievous Josh Greene grin. "Yeah," he said. "Wanna make something of it?"

"No," I said. "I just wondered."

He looked around the table and asked, "Where do I sit?"

"Wherever you want, I guess."

"I might as well sit next to you," he said. "Just like in school."

"Yeah," I said. "You might as well."

JEANNE BETANCOURT has written many books and screenplays, including *Smile! How to Cope With Braces* and three other novels about Aviva and Josh: *The Rainbow Kid, Turtle Time,* and *Puppy Love.* Her young adult novels include *Not Just Party Girls, Home Sweet Home,* and *Sweet Sixteen and Never . . .* Among her original teleplays for ABC After School Specials are "Supermom's Daughter," "Teen Father," "Don't Touch," and "Tattle." Her work has been nominated for five Emmys and two Humanitas awards. She is the recipient of the National Psychological Association's Award for Excellence in the Media.

Jeanne Betancourt lives in New York City and Connecticut with her husband, Lee Minoff, and a dog named Willie. Her daughter, Nicole—the original Rainbow Kid—is now in college.

Great FREE offer
just for you!

Join SNEAK PEEKS™!

Do you want to know what's new before anyone else? Do you like to read great books about girls just like you? If you do, then you won't want to miss SNEAK PEEKS! Be the first of your friends to know what's hot ... When you join SNEAK PEEKS™, we'll send you FREE inside information in the mail about the latest books ... *before they're published!* Plus updates on your favorite series, authors, and exciting new stories filled with friendship and fun ... adventure and mystery ... girlfriends and boyfriends.

It's easy to be a member of SNEAK PEEKS™. Just fill out the coupon below ... and get ready for fun! It's FREE! Don't delay—sign up today!

Skylark is Riding High with Books for Girls Who Love Horses!

☐ **A HORSE OF HER OWN by Joanna Campbell**
15564-4 $2.75
Like many 13-year-olds, Penny Rodgers has always longed to ride a horse. Since her parents won't pay for lessons, Penny decides to try her hand at training an old horse named Bones. When she turns him into a champion jumper, Penny proves to everyone that she's serious about riding!

☐ **RIDING HOME by Pamela Dryden**
15591-1 $2.50
Betsy Lawrence has loved horses all her life, and until her father's remarriage, was going to get her own horse! But now there's just not enough money. And Betsy can't help resenting her new stepsister Ferris, who is pretty, neat, does well in school, and gets all the music lessons she wants—Ferris loves music the way Betsy loves horses. Can the two girls ever learn to be sisters—and even friends?

New Series!

☐ **HORSE CRAZY: THE SADDLE CLUB: BOOK #1 by Bonnie Bryant**
15594-6 $2.95 Coming in September
Beginning with HORSE CRAZY: BOOK #1, this 10-book miniseries tells the stories of three very different girls with one thing in common: horses! Fun-loving Stevie and serious Carole are at Pine Hollow Stables for their usual lesson, when they meet another 12-year-old named Lisa. Her elaborate riding outfit prompts the girls to play a practical joke on her. After Lisa retaliates a truce is formed, and so is THE SADDLE CLUB! Look for HORSE SHY: BOOK #2, Coming in October!

GOOD NEWS! The five best friends who formed the AGAINST TAFFY SINCLAIR CLUB will be starring in a series all their own.

IT'S NEW. IT'S FUN. IT'S FABULOUS. IT'S THE FABULOUS FIVE!

From Betsy Haynes, the bestselling author of the Taffy Sinclair books, *The Great Mom Swap*, and *The Great Boyfriend Trap*, comes THE FABULOUS FIVE. Follow the adventures of Jana Morgan and the rest of THE FABULOUS FIVE as they begin the new school year in Wakeman Jr. High.

☐ SEVENTH-GRADE RUMORS (Book #1)

The Fabulous Five are filled with anticipation, wondering how they'll fit into their new class at Wakeman Junior High. According to rumors, there's a group of girls called The Fantastic Foursome, whose leader is even prettier than Taffy Sinclair. Will the girls be able to overcome their rivalry to realize that rumors aren't always true? 15625-X $2.75

☐ THE TROUBLE WITH FLIRTING (Book #2)

Melanie Edwards insists that she *isn't* boy crazy. She just can't resist trying out some new flirting tips from a teen magazine on three different boys—her boyfriend from her old school, a boy from her new school, and a very cute eighth-grader! 15633-0 $2.75/$3.25 in Canada

☐ THE POPULARITY TRAP (Book #3)

When Christie Winchell is nominated for class president to run against perfect Melissa McConnell from The Fantastic Foursome, she feels pressure from all sides. Will the sudden appearance of a mystery candidate make her a winner after all? 15634-9 $2.75

HER HONOR, KATIE SHANNON (Book #4)

When Katie Shannon joins Wakeman High's new student court, she faces the difficult job of judging both her friends and foes. On Sale: December 15640-3 $2.75

Watch for a brand new book each and every month!

Book #5 On Sale: January/Book #6 On Sale: February

YOUR OWN

SLAM BOOK!

If you've read *Slambook Fever*, Sweet Valley High #48, you know that slam books are the rage at Sweet Valley High. Now *you* can have a slam book of your own! Make up your own categories, such as "Biggest Jock" or "Best Looking," and have your friends fill in the rest! There's a four-page calendar, horoscopes and questions most asked by Sweet Valley readers with answers from Elizabeth and Jessica

It's a must for SWEET VALLEY fans!

☐ 05496 FRANCINE PASCAL'S SWEET VALLEY HIGH
        SLAM BOOK
        Laurie Pascal Wenk $3.50

- -